TRASH TALK

As Davis landed, the tough guy guarding him pushed him to the floor.

"What are you doing, man?" Davis shouted as he scrambled to his feet. "You undercut me!"

"Want to make something of it?" the player yelled back.

Suddenly the other members of the opposing team ran up and surrounded Davis. One of them, the point guard, shoved Davis in the chest. Davis staggered backward and was quickly pinned against the wall of the gym.

"Five against one isn't very fair," Joe said as he burst through the players around Davis. With a leap and a flying tackle, Joe knocked a big guy to the ground. Stepping in right behind his brother, Frank stood shoulder to shoulder with Davis.

"Back off!" Frank yelled. "We beat you—now get over it."

Books in THE HARDY BOYS CASEFILES™ Series

Available from ARCHWAY Paperbacks

THE HARDY BOYS

CASEFILES™

NO. 107

FAST BREAK

FRANKLIN W. DIXON

AN ARCHWAY PAPERBACK
Published by POCKET BOOKS
New York London Toronto Sydney Tokyo Singapore

This book is a work of fiction. Names, characters, places and incidents are products of the author's imagination or are used fictitiously. Any resemblance to actual events or locales or persons, living or dead, is entirely coincidental.

AN ARCHWAY PAPERBACK *Original*

 An Archway Paperback published by
POCKET BOOKS, a division of Simon & Schuster Inc.
1230 Avenue of the Americas, New York, NY 10020

Copyright © 1996 by Simon & Schuster Inc.
Produced by Mega-Books, Inc.

ISBN: 0-671-50430-4

First Archway Paperback printing January 1996

10 9 8 7 6 5 4 3 2 1

THE HARDY BOYS, AN ARCHWAY PAPERBACK and colophon are registered trademarks of Simon & Schuster Inc.

THE HARDY BOYS CASEFILES is a trademark of Simon & Schuster Inc.

Cover photograph from "The Hardy Boys" series © 1995 Nelvana Limited/Marathon Productions S.A. All Rights Reserved.

The logo design is ™ and copyright © 1995 Nelvana Limited.

Printed in the U.S.A.

IL 6+

FAST BREAK

Chapter

1

"GREAT GAME, HUH?" Frank Hardy yelled excitedly over the din of fifteen thousand frenzied basketball fans.

"College hoops at its finest, Packard and Bayport U.," agreed Frank's friend Davis Johns, who was seated next to him. "The teams are great," he added just as a Packard College player slam-dunked and a roar burst out from the fans.

Frank took in the crowd packed into the airy, brightly lit gymnasium. It seemed that every eye was trained on the court and the ten players.

"I can't think of a better way to spend Presidents' Week vacation than watching college league playoffs," Frank said. "Right, Joe?" He nudged his blond-haired younger brother, who he caught glancing down the sidelines. "And can you believe these courtside seats?"

"Awesome," Joe murmured absently.

"I think Joe has his mind on something other than basketball," Davis commented, gesturing toward the cheerleaders.

Frank laughed, then turned back to Davis. "Do you think you want to come here to play ball or go to Bayport?"

Davis turned his handsome light brown face away from the court action and toward Frank for a moment. "It's tempting to come here," he answered. "Packard fans really do support B-ball. I mean, it's the biggest sport on campus. Coach Trevanian promised me that if I do go here, I'll get lots of playing time, too."

Davis was the star basketball player for Bayport High. Frank knew that dozens of colleges across the country were recruiting him heavily. Davis had narrowed his choices to either Packard or Bayport University. Because his mom and dad, who ran a card shop in Bayport, were away at a trade show, Davis had asked Frank and Joe to accompany him as he visited the two schools this week. Right then, he and the Hardys were guests of the Packard College team.

"I'll say this, Davis. The campus sure has its attractions," Joe commented wryly.

"Get off it, Joe. Davis has more to think

2

about than cheerleaders. Choosing a college to play for is a big step."

"You're right, Frank," Davis said. "I want to make sure the school I sign with has all the things I want. And I'm not just talking about hoops. It's got to have a strong academic reputation and not treat athletes like dumb jocks. I'm still planning on being a premed major."

"I hope you have time for all the classes," Joe said.

"I'll make the time," Davis assured him. He stood up and stretched his tall, lean frame for a minute. Folding chairs weren't built for someone six feet seven inches. "I'll tell you one thing, though," he added, sitting down again, his eyes back on the court. "I can compete with these guys. I know I can play college ball."

"No question." Frank smiled. "You were voted the best high school player in the whole state."

"Thanks for the encouragement," Davis said. "I knew there was a reason I asked you to come with me on this trip. Seriously, though, you're really helping me get a feel for these schools. Coaches and recruiters can fill your head with more questions than answers."

"No problem," Frank responded above the roar of the crowd when Packard hit a three-pointer. "Anyway, we should be thanking *you*— you're the one who got us tickets to a sold-out game and a vacation at 'beautiful Packard College.' "

Time was called by Bayport, and the crowd quieted again.

"This place *is* pretty nice, isn't it?" Davis said. "I can't believe it's only forty miles from Bayport."

"And don't forget we still get to have great seats for the next playoff game between these two at Bayport," Joe added.

"These two games are going to settle one of the closest league championship playoffs ever," Frank said. "I wouldn't put money on either game if I was a millionaire."

The referee blew his whistle, signaling play to resume. Glancing up at the scoreboard, Frank saw that the game was now tied at 78. The noise in the gym was deafening, with everyone stomping, yelling, and clapping. The Bayport Lancers brought the ball upcourt. Packard was playing a pressing man-on-man defense. The Bayport guard's pass went out-of-bounds. The fans cheered as Packard got the ball and called a time-out to talk strategy. As the players walked to their respective benches, Davis and the Hardys could hear both coaches screaming.

"I see why they call him Stormin' Norman," Frank said, nudging Davis. "Just look at him."

The Bayport coach, Norman Whiteside, was yelling at the guard who had thrown the ball out-of-bounds. Whiteside's face was red, and the veins in his forehead appeared to be ready to burst.

"You're out, Turbo," Frank heard the coach yell. "I'm not going to let you cost us another game. Get to the bench."

Frank watched the player, who had a slim but very muscular build, stalk to the far end of the bench. The player turned and opened his mouth to yell back at the coach, but one of the assistants restrained him. Still, Frank thought, Stormin' Norman couldn't mistake the venom in the player's eyes.

"If looks could kill." Frank whistled softly.

Joe nodded. "Isn't he one of their best players?" he asked, leaning over to Davis.

Davis nodded. "That's Tommy 'Turbo' Thomson."

Davis's voice was almost lost as the coach worked his way down the bench, yelling at every player.

"Whiteside *is* a terror," Frank said.

"What?" Davis said, his attention focused on the coach. "Oh, yeah. A real drill sergeant. But he does make great players. Lots of them go on to the pros. Whiteside has led Bayport to ten league titles and a national championship. His coaching could give me the edge I need to take my game to the pro level."

5

"But would you be able to put up with his bullying?" Frank asked.

"That's the million-dollar question," Davis responded. "But I'll learn more about Whiteside and the Bayport program when I visit them next."

Play resumed and the Packard point guard dribbled toward the key. Spotting a teammate close in, he passed the ball. The forward grabbed the ball and with a quick two-step hop launched himself toward the basket. The Bayport player defending him knocked the Wildcat to the ground hard as the shot bounced off the rim. One of the refs blew his whistle to signal a foul. The stadium erupted with Packard fan boos. The Packard player got up from the floor, yelling.

Frank slid to the edge of his seat as the Packard and Bayport players squared off to fight. The three referees ran between the would-be combatants, and both coaches stormed onto the court. The roar of the crowd grew louder.

"Pretty wild, huh?" Joe said to Frank.

"Yeah, go to a basketball game, and it turns into a boxing match right before your eyes," Frank retorted. "Look at the coaches," he said, pointing at the two men, each screaming an inch from the other's face. "I think they're ready to slug it out."

"Those two hate each other," Davis said.

"With their teams usually ranked one and two in the state, the games they play against each other are real grudge matches."

Gradually the referees were able to restore order, and the two coaches were sent back to their benches.

"Whiteside and Trevanian are even fighting over you," Frank commented.

"Yeah," Davis said, managing a laugh. "It's all part of the recruiting wars. I'll tell you, I hate being in the middle of their squabbling. When we talk, they spend more time bad-mouthing each other than discussing the merits of their own programs."

Just then the shrill singing of the referee's whistle brought the three of them back to the game. The Packard player was lined up to take his foul shots. A hush settled over the crowd. Only twenty seconds remained in the game, and the score was still tied at 78.

"I never thought thousands of people could be so quiet," Frank whispered, still on the edge of his seat.

The referee tossed the ball to the Packard player, who bounced the ball once, twice, and then a third time. Keeping his focus on the basket, he raised the ball chest high and shot. The ball floated toward the net and softly slid through.

The fans went crazy.

At the line for his second free throw, the Packard player went through the same routine—three bounces of the ball, a deep breath, and then the shot. Swish! The shot was good, and Packard led by two. A Bayport player signaled for time as the fans erupted in cheers.

While the Packard pep squad led the hometown fans in a victory chant, Frank turned to Davis. "What do you think Coach Whiteside is going to do? Go for a two-point shot to tie the game or a three-pointer to win?"

"My guess would be the three-pointer," Davis answered. "That number thirteen for Bayport can hit from long range."

"We'll soon see if your coaching is as good as your playing," Joe kidded. "Here come the players back on the court."

The fans were wild now, screaming to encourage their Wildcats and distract the Bayport Lancers. Bayport got the ball from the referee at half-court. Frank watched the clock tick down from twelve seconds to eleven to ten as the Bayport point guard dribbled downcourt.

Near the basket, two Packard players tightened around Bayport number thirteen. As the point guard ran around them, he sent a pass in Thirteen's direction. Frank's eyes were glued on Thirteen as the ball reached his hands. Again Frank glanced at the scoreboard to check the time. Everything seemed to be happening in slow motion. Five seconds. Four seconds.

Bayport Thirteen squared his shoulders to the basket, raised his arms to shoot, and jumped. The Packard defender's arms were outstretched, reaching to block the shot.

Frank held his breath as the ball was launched. The rotation was perfect. Two seconds . . . one second. For that split second, the arena was perfectly silent, every fan in the place intently watching the ball float toward the hoop.

Chapter

2

THE SHOT WAS GOOD! Bayport had won. The Packard arena was silent except for the few Bayport fans, players, and coaches who were dancing and yelling jubilantly. Caught up in the excitement of the moment, Joe jumped up in his seat and let out a roar. "Awright, Lancers!"

"Tone it down, Joe," Frank cautioned, glancing over at the Wildcat bench. "After all, we are guests of the Packard team."

"Okay," Joe agreed. "But the Bayport guys are really celebrating this win. Look." Joe pointed to midcourt, where the Bayport players were slapping high fives and congratulating Thirteen for his winning shot. On the court, a TV announcer was interviewing Coach Whiteside. The Packard crowd began to boo. Frank reminded himself that this was no ordinary game for the fans. With the league championship at stake, Packard would have to win at Bayport.

Meanwhile, Coach Trevanian and the Packard team began walking across the court to the locker room exit. A team official motioned to the guys and Frank rose, stretching out his six-foot one-inch frame. He nudged Davis, who stood up, dwarfing Frank and Joe.

"I think that Packard official wants us to join him," Frank said. Joe got up, and the three left their seats. Just ahead of them Frank watched Trevanian storm past Whiteside, who was still talking with the TV sportscaster.

"Nice game, Pete," Frank heard the Bayport coach say, extending his hand to Trevanian. Whiteside sure is a pussycat when he wins, Frank thought. The coach's gray hair and smile made him seem almost grandfatherly.

"Get your hand out of my face, cheater!" Coach Trevanian growled. Frank stopped short. He was now standing next to the two coaches and the sportscaster. Davis and Joe were right behind him.

"Why, you little twerp, I'll . . ." Frank saw Coach Whiteside's face turn deep red. Whiteside reached for Trevanian, cocking his fist back to throw a roundhouse punch. With little time to think, Frank leaped between the two coaches and grabbed Whiteside. Joe stepped up and held a livid Trevanian around the waist to keep him back.

"What's this about cheating?" the sportscaster asked. He thrust his microphone at Trevanian, who was struggling to get out of Joe's strong grasp.

Suddenly players from both teams rushed to the group. A fight erupted as team members jumped to protect their respective coaches. In the middle of the melee, Frank and Joe continued to keep the coaches separated but only barely.

"Call me a cheater? I'll break your scrawny neck," Whiteside screamed as he strained to grab Trevanian.

"Shut up, old man," Trevanian retorted. "You should have retired years ago!"

Frank felt a sharp jab in his shoulder. He turned. It was the sportscaster. He was trying to stick a microphone between the two coaches.

"Coach Trevanian," Frank heard the sportscaster yell, "how is Coach Whiteside a cheater?"

"Get him out of here!" Trevanian screamed, pointing at the sportscaster. A security guard pushed the TV man away.

Frank scanned the court. He saw fans pouring onto the floor, some taunting the Bayport players. Fights had broken out all over. Out of the corner of his eye, Frank noticed a stream of men in dark blue jackets coming out of one of the tunnels at court level. "More security," he yelled at Joe, motioning with his head.

"Finally," Joe shouted back, still wrestling with Trevanian.

Davis had been separated from the Hardys when the initial group of fans surged out of the stands. Now Joe saw his buddy surrounded by some Packard rooters. Joe could hear them threaten Davis for being a Bayport supporter.

"We heard your buddy cheer for Bayport. Let's see how loud you yell now!" Joe heard someone scream at Davis. He handed Trevanian over to a security guard, then ran toward his friend.

"Give it a rest," Joe yelled as he wiggled his way to Davis's side. Not liking the odds now, the Packard rooters backed off.

"Thanks, Joe," Davis said. "The last thing I needed was to get involved in a brawl."

"No problem," Joe said.

He could hear the announcer asking for calm. Joe and Davis made their way back toward Frank and the struggling coaches. In a few moments, campus security guards had formed circles around the players, protecting them from the fans—and one another. Most everyone had calmed down, but not Trevanian or Whiteside.

Frank and a couple of burly security men still had their hands full keeping the two coaches from slugging each other. Even as the security guards escorted Trevanian toward the tunnel leading to the Packard locker room, Frank and Joe heard him threaten Whiteside again.

"That's it, Whiteside," Trevanian taunted. "I'm going to spill the beans on you." He shook off the security guard's grip and moved slowly toward the exit tunnel.

Frank tightened his hold on Coach Whiteside, thinking the man would get even more crazed. To his surprise, Whiteside only smiled.

"Go ahead, you little weasel! But if you do, your career will be over. Or don't you remember Endicott?" The rest of his words were lost in the noise of the crowd as Whiteside turned toward the Bayport locker room. "It's all right, son," he said to Frank. "You can let go. I made my point."

Surprised, Frank released the coach and glanced at Trevanian. Trevanian had turned toward the Bayport coach and gone deathly pale. After a second of silent staring, he headed for his locker room.

Within minutes of the coaches' leaving, order was restored in the stadium and fans began to file out of the arena peacefully. Frank, Joe, and Davis followed the Packard team through the tunnel to their locker room.

14

"Are you guys okay?" Frank asked as the three walked past a bulletin board and drinking fountain. "Those Packard fans looked like they were ready to give it to you."

"We're fine." Joe nodded ruefully.

"How would it have looked if I'd been caught decking a fan?" Davis said, shaking his head.

"Not good," Frank agreed. "But that wouldn't have stopped my brother here." He patted Joe on the back.

"You know me, Frank." Joe laughed sheepishly. "Always ready to mix it up a bit."

The Hardys and Davis reached the Packard locker room, an open doorway in the middle of the concrete hallway. They could hear Coach Trevanian yelling at his players, berating them for losing. As the three were about to enter, the locker room door was shut in their faces. A security guard stepped in front of it, barring their way.

"You're to wait here," the guard said.

"But this is Davis Johns, a recruit," Frank began, pointing at his friend.

"I don't care if he's Michael Jordan. I've got my orders," the guard growled.

"The way the coach is screaming, I wouldn't want to be in there anyway," Joe muttered.

After a few minutes the locker room door was opened. Coach Trevanian, trailed by an assistant, rushed past. Davis tried to catch his attention, but Trevanian was oblivious to anyone. Trevanian's assistant signaled for the guys to follow him.

Davis and the Hardys followed Trevanian and the assistant down the hall to a door labeled Press Room. Entering ahead of Joe and Davis, Frank saw Coach Whiteside standing at a podium. Rows of reporters sat around the room in folding chairs. Frank grabbed three empty seats in the back.

"Over here, guys," Frank motioned. Joe and Davis slid into the seats next to Frank.

"We look forward to the next game at Bayport," they heard Whiteside say in response to a reporter's question. "We don't foresee any new strategies. See you all on Wednesday." The Bayport coach left the podium and made his way toward the door. Then the Packard coach headed up to the podium to begin his postgame press conference. As the two coaches passed in the aisle, Frank clearly felt the animosity between the two.

"Coach T, Coach T, I've got a question!" someone called out. All eyes turned toward the middle of the room. Even Coach Whiteside paused in the doorway. Frank saw that the question came from the reporter who'd been caught in the middle of the on-court melee.

"Yes?" Trevanian had reached the podium.

"Tell us why you called Coach Whiteside a cheater out on the court."

The room fell silent.

Frank's eyes jumped from Trevanian to Whiteside.

Trevanian looked stunned.

Whiteside, who had stepped back into the room, was livid. "Go ahead, hotshot," he shouted at Trevanian. "Spit it out!"

Chapter

3

ALL EYES IN THE ROOM had shifted toward Coach Whiteside. "Go ahead, Trevanian, the reporter wants an answer."

Turning toward the podium, Frank saw that Trevanian was straining to remain calm. The short, dark-haired man's pointy features were tightened into sharp lines and angles. Both his hands were gripping the podium tightly.

The reporter repeated his question. "Do you have anything on Coach Whiteside or not?"

"I didn't mean anything by what I said," Trevanian began haltingly. "The coach is a legend," he added through gritted teeth. "And his program is beyond reproach." Trevanian stepped away from the podium and tried to walk down the aisle, but a crowd of reporters blocked his way.

"Is Whiteside paying off players?" a reporter asked.

"Leave it alone. The press conference is over!" Trevanian exclaimed, elbowing his way through the throng of reporters.

"Coach T!" the first sportscaster to ask a question shouted.

By this time Trevanian and Whiteside were standing side by side at the door, facing the reporters.

"Do you have any worries about security for the next game?"

"I can assure you, gentlemen," Coach Whiteside interjected, "that Coach Trevanian and the Packard team will be well treated when they come to Bayport. We've got a brand-new athletics department dorm for them to stay in, and I can promise you a clean game from my players—not to mention good security."

Trevanian, the shorter of the two, raised his eyes to Whiteside with a sarcastic grin. "Coach Whiteside's newfound hospitality is certainly appreciated," Trevanian snarled, "but the next game will be a war!" With that, Trevanian stomped out of the room.

"Show's over, folks," Whiteside said, waving to the reporters. "See you in Bayport!"

Frank's eyes followed the coach as he sauntered out of the press room. "Whiteside seemed pretty smug for someone who was just accused of cheating," he murmured.

"I'll say," Joe replied as he, Frank, and Davis filed out of the room. The three followed several reporters to the parking lot.

"I just don't know what to make of all this," Davis said as he and the Hardys got into the van to head back to their motel. The room Packard had rented for Davis was big enough for Frank and Joe to crash in with their friend.

Joe maneuvered the van out of the lot and onto the highway.

"This must be hard for you, Davis," Frank said. He was seated next to his brother in the front of the van but had turned to face his friend. "All of a sudden neither Packard nor Bayport looks all that enticing."

"You're not kidding," Davis replied, frowning. "I definitely don't want to get involved in any tainted basketball program. If Whiteside's cheating somehow—maybe paying off players to come to Bayport—his program could be investigated and sanctioned."

"What do you mean?" Joe asked as he steered the van through the traffic.

"It's one way the College Basketball Association keeps schools honest. They prohibit programs found guilty of illegal activities from offering scholarships—which stops teams from getting the best players."

"I get it," Joe said. "Like when colleges pay players money under the table to come to play for them."

"Illegal recruitment," Frank added glumly.

"Exactly," Davis continued. "Sanctioned schools are not allowed to appear in postseason tournaments or on TV. And that costs the schools plenty. A tournament championship school can earn an athletic department over a million dollars."

"Wow!" Frank exclaimed.

"If you ask me," Joe said, "Trevanian was just blowing smoke. If he had had proof of Whitside's cheating, he would have exposed him at the press conference. I think *he's* the underhanded one."

Joe was pulling the van into the motel parking lot. The buff-colored, three-story building was located just off the main highway.

"But," Frank began, "maybe Trevanian spoke out of turn because of the pressure of the game. Maybe he was just burned out and said more than he meant to. You know, Davis, you can't let one isolated incident cloud your view of Packard. You said yourself Packard looks like a great place to go to school."

"I know, Frank," Davis answered, his smooth

forehead creased. From the tone of Davis's voice, Frank could tell his buddy wasn't convinced.

After Joe parked the van and shut off the engine, he and the other two got out and walked to the lobby.

"Let's grab some dinner in the motel coffee shop," Frank said, trying to sound cheerful.

"From the noise my stomach's making, that sounds like a good idea," Joe added.

"Sure," Davis said quietly.

After they were seated in the small, brightly lit coffee shop and had ordered burgers all around, Frank turned to Davis.

"Listen, Davis, I've got a suggestion," he began. "You ought to confront Trevanian when you meet him tomorrow morning. If you have any questions about his coaching or his accusation about Whiteside, you're entitled to some answers."

"You're right," Davis agreed, the spark returning to his eye.

Just then the waitress arrived with the food.

"But that can wait till tomorrow," Joe said. "For now, let's eat!"

The next morning while Joe was still sleeping in, Frank and Davis were sitting with Coach Trevanian in his office. The exasperated look on Davis's face told Frank that the meeting was not going to his friend's liking.

"Coach Trevanian," Davis said, "I appreciate the information about the Packard gym and the proposed renovation of the arena, but I'd like to hear more about the team's relationship with the academic departments."

He took a breath and then continued. "What's the graduation rate of your athletes? Do you have any special minority programs? Will I be able to handle a full premed course load if I play ball for you?"

"Yes, yes, of course," Trevanian assured Davis, nodding his slick-haired head. "The athletic department takes great pride in supporting its scholar athletes."

"Look, sir," Davis began again. "I—"

"None of this 'sir' stuff," Coach Trevanian interrupted, his thin lips spreading into a smile. "Call me Coach."

"All right, Coach." Davis took a deep breath. "Let me lay it on the line. I like Packard. The campus is beautiful, and the students I've met have been extremely helpful. Your basketball program is obviously top rate. But I am concerned about a few things." Davis paused for a second to gather his thoughts.

"Go ahead, Davis. You can be frank with me," Coach Trevanian coaxed.

"Well, Coach, you really did seem to lose it out there on the court yesterday. I'm not sure how I'd fit in with that type of coaching style."

23

Coach Trevanian frowned. "It certainly wasn't my finest hour, I'll admit that. But that was an intense game. You know that Packard and Bayport are heated rivals. I just got carried away."

Scanning his friend's face, Frank saw that Davis was still skeptical. "What about your accusations against the Bayport coach?" Frank asked carefully.

Trevanian glared at Frank but kept his composure. "Simply theatrics for the media," Trevanian said. The coach turned in his chair and stared out the window for a second, apparently lost in his own thoughts. Then he rose from his desk and walked the guys to the door. "I hope to hear from you soon, Davis. As I said earlier, I'm ready to make you a star."

"You will, sir," Davis replied, "hear from me."

He and Frank were halfway out the door when Trevanian added in a surprisingly harsh tone, "You'd be dumber than your grades suggest if you said no."

Out in the hall, with the door to Coach Trevanian's office closed behind them, Frank whistled.

Davis had gone pale.

"That was weird," Frank finally said.

"Yeah," Davis agreed. "It almost sounded like a threat."

Chapter

4

"What's down this way, Coach Brundige?" Davis asked the tall man standing next to him and the Hardys. The four of them were in a well-lit, carpeted hallway in Bayport University's athletic complex. The Hardys and Davis had driven to the school after leaving Packard and making a quick stop for lunch at the Hardys' house.

It was now midafternoon, and Stan Brundige, one of the Bayport Lancers' assistant basketball coaches, was taking them on a tour of the school's new athletic complex.

"To give you some idea of the layout," Coach Brundige answered, "we're in the main corridor where you'll find three coaches' offices—right next to the front entrance. Coach Whiteside has the first office there. Down the corridor, to the right, is the exercise and weight room," Brundige said, pointing. "Let's head that way."

He led the way as they walked past the weight room. Frank noted the new paint on the walls and the modern exercise equipment. It was certainly different from Packard's much older facilities. Brundige stopped at a door marked Construction: No Exit.

"Before you play ball, I want to show you what's going on out here." Brundige held the door open as Davis and the Hardys passed outside onto a gravel walkway. The Hardys and Davis squinted as their eyes adjusted to the bright sunlight.

"Looks impressive," Frank said as he stared at a large construction site with buildings at various stages of completion.

"This addition should be finished before you arrive in the fall, Davis. It will house a new practice court and locker rooms for the basketball and football teams," Brundige said proudly. "The lockers will connect through a series of tunnels already built under the main arena on your left. Those older parts of the complex there," he said, gesturing to three forlorn-looking buildings about a hundred yards from them, "will be torn down to make room for the new facility."

"Bayport obviously takes care of its athletes," Joe said. "What do you think, Davis?" he added, nodding toward his friend.

"I like it," Davis admitted. "But right now, I wouldn't mind giving the old hardwood a try. Can we play a little?" Davis asked, turning to Brundige.

"Sure. I'll get you a couple of lockers and some practice sweats. Follow me." Brundige led the group back into the athletic complex. Passing the coaches' offices on the main corridor, the group headed down another hallway in the opposite direction from the weight room. The guys found themselves at the entrance to a huge, dark, barnlike room. A few games were being played on the three basketball courts that ran the length of the gym floor.

"A bit gloomy, I admit." Brundige smiled. "But the new practice gym will be great." Brundige pointed to his left. "The lockers are right through there. A gym monitor will lend you some gear. I told some of the gym-rat regulars that you'd be coming down. Just introduce yourselves and they'll let you have the next game. I've got some calls to make, but I'll be back." Brundige began walking away.

"Oh, I almost forgot," Brundige said as he turned back toward Davis and the Hardys. He reached into his shirt pocket and pulled out three plastic cards. "We had these identification cards made for you." He handed them to Frank, who took his and passed the other two to Davis and Joe. "They'll let you into any facility on campus. Now, I really have got to run."

"Thanks, Coach," Davis said. "Come on, guys, let's get changed and play some hoops."

"I'll catch you guys later. B-ball isn't exactly my game," Joe said as Frank and Davis ducked into the locker room. "I saw a sign that says the gym closes at eight o'clock. How about if I meet you in front then? In the meantime, I'm going to explore."

"Okay. See you then." Frank waved goodbye.

"Here, man!" Davis shouted at Frank as he sprinted upcourt. Dribbling down the middle of the court, Frank led a fast break toward the basketball hoop. Spotting Davis streaking down the right side of the court, he lofted a perfect pass over the outstretched hand of the defender who was a step behind Davis.

Davis caught the ball at the foul line as a second defender raced in to guard him. Davis faked right and with one dribble to the left, he left the defender grasping nothing but air. Launching himself into the air, Davis stuffed the ball through the hoop. As he landed, he yelled, "Game!"

Frank, who had stopped midcourt after tossing the ball to Davis, pumped his fist excitedly.

28

He ran toward his friend, who was catching his breath on the sidelines.

"Nice shot, Davis," Frank said as he and his friend high-fived each other.

"You're the man, my friend!" one opponent said as he bent over the water fountain for a drink.

"Thanks," Davis said, smiling broadly.

"Hey, Davis," someone called from the bleachers. It was the assistant coach Brundige. "Nice game. And you, too, Hardy!" Brundige stepped down from the bleachers and walked over to the guys. Frank hadn't noticed him earlier.

"Thanks, Coach," Frank gasped. He wiped the sweat from his forehead and bent over, holding his stomach. "I don't suppose you need a short, slow-footed point guard, do you?" he added between deep breaths.

"Not really." Brundige smiled. "But Davis here is another story. We'd love to have you with us, son. Why don't you play a few more games and then we can have a chat about the Bayport program?"

"Sure," Davis said. "Come on, Frank," Davis added, turning to his friend, who was still doubled over next to him. "It's our court. We won the game."

"I'll pass," Frank said, and laughed. "I don't

have the wind you do. You barely broke a sweat."

Frank took a bleacher seat next to Coach Brundige and watched as Davis led his scrimmage team to three consecutive victories. After the last game, Davis walked over to Frank and the coach.

"You looked good out there," Brundige commented. The coach lifted his huge frame off the bleacher seat and stood next to Davis. "I know it's getting a little late, but if you have a few minutes I'd like to tell you a bit about the team."

Frank looked up at a clock on the gym wall. It said seven. "We've got plenty of time, Davis. We don't have to meet Joe for an hour."

"Great," Brundige answered. "Now, Davis, let me tell you about the great opportunity here. Coach Whiteside is looking for a scorer in the front court, someone to play the small forward spot. You'd be perfect, and let me tell you why."

For the next forty-five minutes, Brundige gave Davis the hard sell on Bayport's program. While Davis was paying close attention to the assistant coach, Frank noticed that the gym was emptying out. After a few more minutes, he interrupted, reminding Davis that they had to meet Joe.

"Gee, I'm sorry, guys. I lost track of the

time," Brundige apologized. "And I've got to be somewhere, too," he added, sounding slightly agitated. "But you can't get me to stop when I'm singing the praises of Coach Whiteside. Well, I'll see you tomorrow." Then after a quick glance at his wristwatch, he practically sprinted away.

"We'd better hurry ourselves," Frank said. "Let's wait and shower back at the dorm."

"Agreed," Davis answered as they headed off the gym floor and into the locker room.

After grabbing their stuff from the lockers, they made their way to the front entrance, where a guard was waiting. Frank saw that it was already dark outside. The guard followed them a few steps, then locked the door and walked toward the parking lot.

"You must have had a good time. You're the last ones out of the gym."

Frank looked up to see Joe sitting on a bench under a street lamp.

"Sorry we're late," Davis said, "but Coach Brundige kept us talking forever."

"He really wants you to come to Bayport," Frank commented.

"He made it sound that way," Davis said slowly. "But if Bayport's so gung ho about me, Why didn't Whiteside meet with me? I'm also not sure about Brundige's claim that I'd get a starting position right away. Bayport already has a player, Tommy 'Turbo' Thomson, at small forward. And he made All-Conference his freshman season."

"Hey, if you want to see Coach Whiteside tonight, here's your chance," Frank interjected. "Isn't that his office? A light's on." He pointed toward a row of windows on the ground floor of the gym complex. "Remember, Brundige told us Whiteside had the first office. Let's see if he's in," Frank insisted, walking toward the light.

"I don't know," Davis answered. "We probably can't get back into the building. The doors must be locked."

"This one isn't," Frank replied. He had sprinted past the windows to a side door about seventy-five feet from the main entrance. He held the door open as Joe and Davis walked up to him.

"I really do want to talk to him," Davis said.

The hallways in the athletic department offices were now almost pitch-black, but a beam of light at one side of the corridor indicated that someone was still around. Frank approached the door to the head coach's office, which was slightly ajar, and called out, "Coach Whiteside, hello!"

He got no response. Frank stepped into the secretary's office, followed by Davis and Joe. The light was coming from Coach Whiteside's inner office. Frank moved toward the door.

"Coach?" he said, knocking on the door and pushing it slightly open.

"I don't know about this, Frank," Davis said quietly. "I feel like we're breaking in."

"No problem, Davis," Frank said, turning back toward his friend. "We're just here to see the coach." With that, Frank pushed the door open all the way. He stopped short and let out a sharp gasp.

Sprawled on the floor beside his desk was Coach Whiteside—and he wasn't moving!

Chapter
5

FRANK HURRIED OVER and knelt beside Whiteside.

The coach wasn't breathing.

He reached up to the man's desk, grabbed the phone, and quickly punched in 911. Joe and Davis moved closer to the body.

"Quick, Joe!" Frank shouted. "See if you can find a security guard or anyone. We've got to move fast."

"Right!" Joe yelled as he raced out of the office and into the darkened corridor.

"Hey! Anybody here?" Joe practically screamed.

No one, Joe thought, and turned back. Abruptly he stopped.

Wait a sec. What was that? Joe was staring down the pitch-black corridor that led past the coaches' offices toward the gym.

He stood still for a second, staring. No, I guess it was nothing. I must have just imagined I saw a light.

Joe ran back to Frank and Davis, who had begun administering CPR to the prone man.

"I couldn't find a soul," Joe said.

"Okay," Frank replied tensely. "Paramedics are on the way, but we've started CPR. Why don't you take over for Davis. He's never done this before. Pump his heart while I try to get some air into his lungs."

Using the techniques they had learned in the emergency rescue courses they'd taken, the Hardys administered CPR to the motionless coach. Joe rhythmically pushed on the man's chest as Frank blew air into his mouth.

"No reaction yet," Davis said. "He's still got no pulse!"

Frank raised his head. "One more time, Joe," he said to his brother. Frank bent back down and blew while the younger Hardy pumped the coach's chest, this time harder and more urgently.

Just then two paramedics burst through the doorway into the lighted office followed closely by two campus security guards.

"Step away, fellas," the first paramedic ordered. He straddled Whiteside's body and began pounding on the coach's chest. The other emergency technician put a breathing device on the prone man. "How long has he been like this?" the second EMS guy asked.

"We don't know exactly," Frank said. "But it's been at least five minutes since we found him."

"Okay. Give us some room. We've got to try electric stimulus." The first technician ripped the coach's shirt from his chest and prepped him while the second technician opened the small suitcase he had carried into the office. It had electrodes and a control panel. Flipping on the switch, the technician held the electrodes over the coach.

"Stand clear!"

With a quick movement, the technician pressed the two electrodes to the lifeless body. It jolted.

"Nothing," the other technician said. "No beat or pulse."

"Clear!" The technician pressed the electrodes to the coach again. Again came the sickening jolt.

"I'm still not getting anything!"

"One more time. Clear!" For a third time the technician pressed the electrodes to flesh. But the coach's heart wouldn't start.

"It's no go." The first paramedic shrugged. "He's gone."

Frank and Joe stared at the technician numbly. Davis slumped against a wall, staring at the lifeless body of Coach Whiteside. After a moment Frank put a hand on Davis's shoulder.

"Hang on, man," he said quietly. "I know it's tough. We all did the best we could."

"I know. But I've never seen anyone die right before my eyes."

The coach's office was filling up with people. The paramedics were conferring with two uniformed Bayport police officers as well as the security guards. Frank saw one of the paramedics point in their direction.

One of the Bayport officers walked over to the Hardys and Davis.

"The paramedics tell me you guys made the nine-one-one call," the officer said calmly. He had taken a pad and pencil from his breast pocket. "Can I get your names? I've got a few questions."

"Sure," Frank offered. "It's Hardy. Frank Hardy. This is my brother, Joe. And this is Davis Johns."

"Hmm—Hardy," the officer said. "Fenton's boys, aren't you?" he asked. Most of the Bayport force knew Frank and Joe's father, who was a private investigator. "What are you doing here?"

"We're here with our friend," Joe responded

as he pointed to Davis. "He's being recruited by Bayport U. for their basketball team."

"That's right, Officer," Davis added haltingly. "We just came in to see if the coach had a few minutes to talk. And that's when we saw—" Davis hesitated—"that's when we discovered the coach on the floor."

"I understand," the officer said sympathetically. He closed his notebook. "Thanks for the information. Please stick around for a few more minutes."

Frank nodded. Just then two men burst into Coach Whiteside's office. Both appeared breathless. Frank recognized one as the assistant coach Brundige. The other he didn't know. He was short—around five feet eight inches, Frank decided—and had dark hair.

"What happened?" the man demanded to no one in particular. Seeing the coach's body on the floor, he gasped. "Why aren't you doing anything?" he yelled at the paramedics, who were in the process of packing up their gear.

"Sorry," one of them said. "We tried everything."

The officer who'd been interviewing Davis and the Hardys moved over to the man. "Sir, can I get your name? Did you know the coach?" the officer asked.

"I'm Coach Zabella. Eddie Zabella. And this

is Coach Brundige," the man offered quietly. "We are—or were—Whiteside's assistants."

Coach Brundige stepped up next to Zabella. "What happened, Officer? Was it a heart attack? He was taking pills for a heart condition," Brundige explained excitedly. "We all told him to take it easy. But he just wouldn't listen."

Frank watched Brundige fidget nervously, while Zabella continued to stare angrily at the paramedics.

"It does look like his heart gave out," one of the paramedics said as the police officers ushered everyone out of the coach's office.

"We still have to check it out," the officer answered. "Are you boys staying on campus?" he added. "We'll need to interview you further. Strictly routine, but we'll need to talk."

"Sure—" Frank began.

"We've put them up in the new athletic dorm," Coach Brundige interrupted. "In fact, if you don't mind, I'll escort them over there now."

"That's fine," the officer responded. "Just one question, though, Mr. Brundige. Did you see anything unusual? You and Mr. Zabella must have been around the gym, since you arrived here only a few minutes after we did."

"I, um—was in my car in the parking lot when I saw the ambulance speed past," Brundige said. "I was worried that it might be Coach Whiteside, what with his condition and all."

"I was here to pick up some game tapes," Coach Zabella offered. "Saw the ambulance and followed you guys in."

"Thanks," the officer said. "You can go. We'll let you and other campus officials know what we find out tomorrow. We'll have to get a coroner in here. And that could take hours."

Coach Brundige turned toward Davis and the Hardys. "Do you need a lift back to the dorm?" he asked calmly. As Frank nodded that they could use a ride, he noticed that the coach seemed to have regained his composure.

"Good idea, Stan," Coach Zabella seconded. "I'll stay here to contact the athletic director."

Brundige ushered Davis and the Hardys down the corridor and out the building through the side door.

"My car's right over here," Brundige said.

They all piled in and after a quick drive, the guys were in the dorm, walking up the stairs to their rooms. The dorm had just been built as part of the new athletic facility expansion program. Only part of it was currently occupied, but Brundige had told them that many Bayport athletes would live in the dorm when it was finished in the fall.

"Here you are, fellas," Coach Brundige said as he opened the door to the suite Davis and the Hardys were sharing. The three of them followed him into the main room of the suite. It was large, with a sofa, chairs, and two writing desks. Doors on either side of the suite opened onto small bedrooms. The boys had already tossed their bags into the rooms.

"If you need anything, just ask the resident assistant. There aren't many people in this wing yet, so it should be quiet. And after what's happened, I'm sure—" Brundige hesitated for a moment. "What I mean to say," he continued, "is if there's anything I can do . . . This has been a shock, and I—"

"Thanks, Coach," Frank quickly interjected. He could see how shaken the man was. In fact, he thought he could see tears forming at the corners of his eyes.

Davis tossed his gym bag onto the couch in the living room. "Will we see you tomorrow?"

"Yes. Either Eddie or I will contact you. I imagine we'll all have to meet with the police and school officials. It'll be hectic, but—"

"We understand," Davis said quietly. "And we appreciate your taking the time to drive us over here."

"Thanks, guys." Brundige managed a small smile. "Listen, you get a good night's rest. Despite everything, we'll give you a good tour of Bayport tomorrow afternoon. Same time. The

41

team wants you here very much, Davis." The coach headed out the door. "Good night."

" 'Night," the guys said in unison. As Joe closed the door behind the coach, Davis let out a long sigh.

"It's been a hard day," Frank said. "Let's get some rest. Try not to think about what happened, Davis. There's nothing more we could have done."

"I know," Davis answered quietly as he headed into his bedroom. "I'll see you in the morning."

"Come on, Davis. I'm starved," Joe shouted. The three had overslept. It was around 11:30 A.M. He and Frank were standing in the doorway to the hall. "You've got to check out the school cafeteria. If the burgers aren't good, you can't play for Bayport."

"Always led by your stomach, huh?" Frank needled.

"I'm coming," Davis answered. He'd been listening to a news report about the coach's death on the portable radio he'd brought. "I've got to grab my wallet. I left it in my gym bag last night."

Davis walked back into his room and when he came out, he had his gym bag in hand. "You know, the news said that Wednesday's game is still on. It's going to be played in the coach's honor—and the athletic director, Ray Crawford, will deliver a eulogy." Davis was still rummaging through his bag as Frank and Joe stepped into the hall.

"What?" Davis began. Then he shouted, "Hey, guys, look at this!"

Frank and Joe turned back toward their friend. Davis had fallen back onto the living room sofa, his mouth open and his eyes wide with surprise. Frank saw that Davis was staring down at the gym bag, which he was holding in his lap.

"What is it?" Frank asked quickly.

"Look at this!" Davis raised his eyes to meet Frank's.

Frank stared at Davis. In his friend's left hand was what appeared to be a letter. And in his right he held ten thousand-dollar bills.

Chapter

6

JOE WHISTLED SOFTLY as he stared at the money. "That's a lot of cash."

"What's the note say?" Frank asked.

"That the money is my first Bayport paycheck," Davis answered in a shaky voice. "And more will follow once I sign with the team."

"Now we know Bayport really wants you," Joe kidded. "This kind of dough could make college fun."

Frank saw Davis wince. "This is serious," Frank chided his brother. "Bribery is illegal."

"He's right, Joe," Davis added worriedly. "If it even vaguely looks like I solicited or accepted this money, it could kill any chance I've got at a college scholarship or pro basketball career.

The CBA is cracking down hard on under-the-table payments to recruits. I've got to do something about this. Give the money to the police or someone."

"Do you think Whiteside sent it?" Frank asked. "Could Trevanian's accusations be true? Was Whiteside recruiting players with cash?"

"That just adds to my problem," Davis answered, pacing the room. "I don't want to come forward with this the day after the coach passed away. It seems mean to question his recruiting policies now that he's gone."

"True enough," Frank agreed. "We don't even know that he was the one who delivered the money."

"I wonder," Joe interjected, "if maybe the money and the coach's death are related."

"Do you think they could be?" Davis asked anxiously.

"Maybe," Joe answered.

"Hold on a second," Frank said, trying to make Davis feel better. "Let's look at the facts."

"We know Whiteside and Trevanian didn't get along," Joe said quickly.

"Right," Frank agreed. "Trevanian certainly seemed to be pointing the finger at Whiteside and his program."

"But how would this all lead to murder?"

45

Davis asked incredulously. "Accusations and bribes are one thing, but—"

"I know it seems far-fetched," Frank began. "But you said yourself that big-time hoops can be a real pressure cooker. And the sports magazines have all done articles about illegal recruiting activities."

"Wait a minute," Joe interrupted, grabbing his head with his hand. "How could I have forgotten! I think I saw someone running out of the gym last night right after we found Whiteside."

"What?" Frank said.

"Yeah," Joe nodded. "While I was in the hall, just before I went back into Whiteside's office I thought I saw a light flash on down the corridor. A shadow seemed to run past. Then it was pitch-black again." He looked carefully at Frank. "I think we've got a case."

"Maybe," Frank said thoughtfully. "But the main thing right now is to figure out what to do about this money."

"We're on the case, then?" Joe asked eagerly. "Well, the first thing to do is investigate the coach's death—"

"Investigate the coach's death?" Davis repeated in surprise.

Frank shot an angry glance at his brother. "The first thing to do," he said calmly, "is to get this money in a safe place. Davis is our first priority." He turned back toward his friend. "How about if we give the money and note to my dad? That way, it will be safe, and we can hold off accusing Whiteside and the Bayport program—"

"And we can start investigating, maybe draw the culprit out," Joe quickly added. "We're perfectly placed to do it."

"But only if you agree, Davis," Frank cut in.

"Maybe," Davis said skeptically. "But if things start getting hairy, I want you to go to the police right away. What'll our first move be?"

"To call my dad," Frank said as he picked up the phone. It was installed in the wall near the suite's door. "I'm going to let him know right now." Frank cradled the phone receiver on his shoulder. "Dad," he said after a few seconds, "it's Frank." He kept his voice as nonchalant as possible. "We've got a little situation here and could use your help."

Frank outlined the story for his father and then was silent. Joe saw Frank nod his head a few times before speaking again.

"Sure, Dad," Frank said. "We'll be careful. We'll go straight to the authorities if things start to get out of hand. Don't worry. Just give us a couple of days."

Joe smiled and rolled his eyes.

" 'Bye, Dad," Frank said at last. "We'll talk to you soon." He hung up the phone.

47

"Dad's being cautious, right?" Joe said.

"Sure is," Frank answered. "But he'll take the money and give us a few days to check things out." Frank turned to Davis.

"Joe and I'll prowl around the campus, ask some questions, and check out the allegations Trevanian made against Whiteside. You just play it cool. Continue your visit here at Bayport."

Davis glanced at his watch. "I guess we should grab something to eat and then keep our appointment with Brundige."

"Yeah," Joe answered. "He could provide some valuable information. Let's roll."

"There's not that much more to tell," Coach Brundige began in answer to Davis's questions about the late coach. "His teams were always winners. We'll all miss him."

Davis, Frank, and Joe were seated in Brundige's office. The walls were plastered with sports pictures, and a trophy case stood behind the coach's desk. Frank noted that the trophies all belonged to Brundige, who'd once been a star player himself.

"Coach," Frank said in a quiet tone, "may I ask a touchy question?"

Brundige leaned forward in his chair and met Frank's eyes. Watching him, Joe tensed a little.

"By all means," Brundige replied.

Frank began slowly. "At the Packard game, Trevanian made some allegations, and we've heard rumors—"

Brundige cut off Frank with a wave of his hand. His voice took on a serious tone. "I'll be honest with you guys," he said. "Whiteside had a few run-ins with players. One time he slapped one of them. The incident led to a lawsuit but was hushed up by some school bigwigs."

Brundige went on. "Years ago rumor had it that Whiteside got some of his best players no-show jobs with local boosters. Nothing was proven, but rumors have a way of dogging coaches in this game."

Brundige offered a quick smile to Davis. "Whatever may have happened in the past, I can personally assure you that Whiteside's program has been clean for as long as I've been here. He was a great coach. And I still think the program could benefit you greatly." Brundige got up from his chair. "But now, guys, I've got to run. We'll have to put off that tour till later. As you can imagine, the team's got a lot to deal with right now."

"Sure, sir," Davis said. He got up from his chair as did Frank and Joe. "We'll see you later. And thanks."

The three put their coats on and left the athletic complex to head back along the tree-lined walkways to their dorm. Frank knew that when the trees leafed out and the grass greened up, the campus would look like a well-manicured park.

Joe stopped abruptly and suggested they about-face to pay a visit to the Bayport coroner's office.

"Won't it be closed?" Davis asked. "It is Sunday, after all."

"Not necessarily," Joe said. "The coroner is always on call. Anyway, we should check it out."

"You guys go ahead," Davis said, deep in thought. "I'd like to walk around the campus a bit."

Frank nodded, knowing it might be good for his friend to spend some time alone. "We'll catch up back at the dorm," he said.

"Did you hear that, Frank?" Joe whispered. The two of them were standing in the Bayport coroner's office, a small room in a nondescript brick building in downtown Bayport. They had arrived a few minutes earlier and were admitted to a waiting room by an assistant who told them to make themselves comfortable until the coroner returned. But left alone, they wandered into the coroner's office and opened a few files left on his desk. Frank noticed the report on Coach Whiteside's death just as Joe spoke.

"That sounds like footsteps. I think some- one's coming!"

The Hardys desperately wanted to speak to the coroner but not like this, when it was obvi- ous that they had been snooping.

For a moment they stood frozen behind the coroner's desk.

"We can't get out the way we came in," Frank whispered.

"But we've got to leave."

"No. Let's just hide," Frank said, scanning the office. "No cover in here," he whispered. He peeked through a door at the rear that was slightly ajar. Through the crack he could see a bank of refrigerated corpse slabs built into the far wall. It was the morgue room. The door to one empty slab was open.

"Joe, move," Frank said urgently, pushing his brother through the door that connected the of- fice with the morgue. Frank pulled the slab by its handle. "Jump on this corpse table. I'll push you into the wall. Hurry!"

Joe turned to his brother. His eyes were wide with disbelief.

"There's no time to argue," Frank answered quickly, pushing his brother up onto the cold metal table. "The coroner will be in here any second. And I've still got to hide!"

Joe scrambled onto the table. "Okay," he said as Frank slid him into his temporary coffin.

"Just remember to get me out when the guy's gone."

"Sure thing," Frank said. "Sweet dreams," he added as he pushed the slab into the wall. He gave Joe a little air by leaving the slab door slightly ajar. Then he turned to find a place to hide himself. All the other slab doors were locked, and the rest of the morgue room offered little cover.

Frank had only seconds. He ran back into the outer office, through the coroner's office, searching the room. In one corner stood a ceiling-high closet he hadn't noticed before. He dashed toward it and jumped in just as the coroner entered the office. Leaving the door open a crack, Frank watched the balding, middle-aged man walk to his desk and leaf through some folders.

After a minute, he appeared to be ready to leave. Frank heaved a silent sigh of relief. He knew Joe must be going batty in the refrigerated coffin.

Then without warning the man slipped out of his line of vision. Frank waited to hear the outer door open—but it didn't.

"Who left this slab door open?" The man's voice cut through the silence. Frank's heart skipped a beat. The coroner was in the morgue room. If he closed the door, Joe could suffocate!

The sickening sound of a slamming door

echoed throughout the morgue room. "That'll do it," the man said out loud. Frank's eyes grew wide as the coroner placed a key in the lock of the door of the morgue.

Frank stifled a horrified gasp. If Frank couldn't get to Joe soon the slab would be his tomb!

Chapter

7

FRANK HELD HIS BREATH. What now? Joe could have only five minutes of air at the most.

He shifted anxiously in his cramped hiding place. If the coroner would only leave, Frank could jimmy the lock. But a quick peek from the closet revealed the man settling in and reading a file folder at his desk.

Frank slowly counted to sixty. When the coroner still didn't move, Frank shook his head. He knew he couldn't wait any longer. He'd have to tell the coroner the truth and risk the consequences.

Frank pushed open the supply closet door, letting in a bit of light. His eyes bulged in surprise. The coroner was no longer at his desk.

So Frank opened the closet door cautiously and peered out. A door was slammed shut and Frank drew his hand back in surprise. Then he heard a key being turned in a lock. It had to be the coroner leaving, he thought.

Frank stepped out of the supply closet and dashed to the morgue room door. Using a paper clip, he jimmied the lock and raced toward Joe's slab door. A banging noise could be heard from the wall.

"I'm coming, Joe!" Frank said urgently. "Just a second." Reaching the slab, Frank gave a quick pull on the door, and the corpse table slid out.

Frank stared down at Joe. His brother lay perfectly still, his eyes closed and his face a deadly shade of white. Frank could feel his heart pounding. "Joe?" he whispered.

Suddenly Joe's eyes popped open and he gasped. "Don't ever," he said between breaths, "do that to me again." He sat up on the table, his chest heaving. "Not much air in there, you know."

Frank helped his brother sit up, and a minute later Joe hopped off the slab. "Had you fooled there for a minute, didn't I?" he said.

"Very funny," Frank replied. "But we'd better get out of here before the coroner comes back."

"If he does, it'll be your turn to jump into the deep freeze."

"You guys had to do what?" Davis asked incredulously. Frank and Joe had just returned to the dorm room and were explaining what had happened to Davis. "Are you all right, Joe?"

Joe plopped down onto the couch. "Fine," he said. "Just your average buried-alive episode."

Davis didn't crack a smile. "This is getting way too dangerous, guys," he exclaimed.

"All in a day's work," Joe said, trying to sound calm. "Unfortunately, we weren't able to read the coroner's report."

"That's right," Frank said. "So there's still a lot we need to find out." Frank went over to the phone. "Dad told us to call."

Joe and Davis sat silently as Frank talked to Fenton Hardy. After a quick back and forth, Frank hung up.

"What did Dad say?" Joe asked.

"He did some checking on his own," Frank answered, glancing from his brother to Davis. "Everybody—including the police, school officials, and the coroner—thinks Whiteside's death was caused by a heart attack."

Joe's eyes lit up. "So the case is ours!"

"You heard Frank," Davis said, turning to

Joe. "There's no case. Whiteside died of a coronary—"

"But someone sent you a bribe," Frank interrupted. "We've got to investigate."

Davis sighed. "All right. What do we do? I'm supposed to watch tomorrow's ten A.M. practice."

"That's perfect," Frank said. "We'll catch practice in the morning, talk to some people, and poke around a bit. Now, let's grab some dinner and make it an early night."

"I'll say one thing," Joe said. "The cafeteria food here is better than I expected." He, Frank, and Davis were just entering the Bayport Arena. They were going to watch the practice. The twelve-thousand-seat arena was practically empty except for the team, coaches, and a few reporters. The Lancers were running drills on the court.

"Flapjacks and syrup. Guess you can't beat that," Davis agreed, smiling.

"Is this okay, Frank?" Davis was pointing at seats about ten rows up from the court. He and Joe were settling in as Frank reached them. "I like to sit back a bit so I can see the whole court. It gives me a better sense of the game," Davis explained as Frank took the seat next to him.

Down on the court the Lancers were starting

a full-court scrimmage. Half the team donned yellow practice jerseys and gathered around Brundige. At the far end of the court the rest of the players were huddled with Eddie Zabella. A whistle blew.

"Okay! Let's do it," the Hardys and Davis heard Zabella shout. "I know we're all down and that's understandable. But we need to prepare for Packard. So, come on, work hard for Coach W!" Frank watched as both groups broke their huddles. Five players from each squad met at center court. Zabella and Brundige were acting as referees.

"This should be interesting," Davis said. "It'll give me a chance to see how Zabella and Brundige handle the team."

"I don't know if I could just play the game as if nothing happened," Joe commented.

"I know what you mean," Davis answered. "But Zabella seems to be using Whiteside's death to motivate the players—or at least some of them."

As the game progressed, Frank could see Davis's eyes following one player up and down the court. Frank noticed that the guy Davis was watching was the small forward—Davis's position.

Just then a whistle blew shrilly.

"Stop!" Coach Brundige shouted, grabbing the ball from the player standing next to him.

"Come on, Turbo!" Brundige yelled, pointing his finger at the player Davis had been staring at so closely. "Guard somebody, will you? Either that or I'll make you sit out."

"I was waiting for that," Davis said quietly as he nudged Frank. "That guy doesn't play any defense. He let his man score three straight times without so much as a handcheck."

Frank watched Turbo bristle. "Why don't you leave me alone!"

"Okay, you're out—" Brundige yelled.

But before he could continue, Coach Zabella intervened.

"It's all right, Turbo. You can stay in the game," he said calmly. "Okay, guys," Zabella added, addressing all the players. "Show's over. Start it up again." Zabella took the ball from Brundige's hands and tossed it into play.

"Wait a second!" Brundige shouted. "What do you mean by putting Turbo back in the game? He's not even trying."

The gym became absolutely silent as everyone stared at the two coaches. Frank saw a sneer twist Turbo's face.

Zabella led Brundige to the sidelines, right below Davis and the Hardys. Brundige didn't say a word, he just stared toward the court.

"I think you should get off Turbo's back," Zabella said. "We'll need him in the game with Packard. And by the way," he added snidely, "you haven't been named head coach, you know."

Zabella began to walk away from Brundige, who continued to stand there, steaming. Meanwhile, the other players were milling around, obviously not ready to resume practice.

"Interesting, huh?" Frank said to Davis.

"The team is in total disarray," he replied.

Just then a whistle blew at the far end of the court. Coach Zabella was gathering the players around him. Frank saw a man in a Bayport warm-up suit standing next to Zabella. Coach Brundige was the last to reach the semicircle that had formed around Zabella and the newcomer.

"Let's move closer so we can hear what's going on," Joe suggested as he rose from his seat. He, Frank, and Davis walked down toward the arena floor.

"Guys," Zabella addressed the team, stealing a quick glance at Brundige, "Mr. Crawford has an announcement to make."

"He's the athletic director," Davis whispered.

"I know Coach Whiteside's death has hit everyone hard," the distinguished-looking man began, "but we've had a terrific season, and I know he'd have wanted you to continue playing to the utmost of your abilities. With that in mind, I'm asking Coach Zabella to take over as head coach on an interim basis."

A murmur went through the crowd, and Frank saw some of the players quietly grumble. Others smiled and clapped. Frank glanced at Brundige. There was a stunned scowl on his face.

"Brundige is totally shocked," Joe whispered. "He can barely contain himself." Frank saw Brundige squeeze both his hands into fists, but the man didn't utter a word.

"Okay, Coach," Crawford said, "the team's all yours." The athletic director started walking off the court. "Good luck on Wednesday, guys," he added as he left.

"Hit the showers, fellas," Zabella said, beaming. "Practice is just about over anyway."

Davis shook his head in disbelief. Frank and Joe followed as he walked toward Brundige.

"It seems a terrible way to treat Coach Brundige," Davis said quietly. "Obviously, Crawford didn't even do him the courtesy of telling him about his decision in advance."

Just then Brundige walked by the three.

"Coach," Davis began, "can we—"

Livid, Brundige brushed past the guys without so much as a glance,then pushed through an exit that led outside.

"Now what?" Joe asked. "Wasn't he going to show us around some more?"

"Maybe Coach Zabella will," Davis suggested.

"I wouldn't count on it," Frank said. He was

pointing back toward the locker room exit. "Zabella's gone. He's probably got the team in the locker room."

"What should we do?" Davis muttered. "I'm beginning to feel abandoned. The team seems to have forgotten we're even here."

"Sorry, my man," Frank said, patting him on the shoulder. "But I've got an idea. If Brundige is gone, then—"

"—we might be able to search his office," Joe finished Frank's sentence for him. "Maybe we'll find something to tie him to the bribe money or even Whiteside's death."

"Let's do it," Frank assented. "We might not get another chance. But first we've got to make sure he's really gone." Joe and Davis followed Frank as he dashed toward the door Brundige had exited.

The door opened directly onto a parking lot reserved for campus personnel. As they stepped into the lot, Frank saw Brundige pull his car out onto the street.

Passing back into the arena, the guys crossed the gym and then went out to the corridor leading to the coaches' offices. Fortunately, it was deserted. The three were standing in front of Coach Brundige's office, two doors down from Whiteside's. Frank motioned Joe and Davis to keep a lookout.

"Watch both ends of the hallway," Frank said quietly. "I'm going in."

"Don't worry," Joe answered. "If anyone comes by we'll just say Davis has an appointment to see Brundige."

Frank tried the knob. It was unlocked. Cautiously he opened the door and peered in. Empty. He stepped in and scanned the office, then walked over to Brundige's desk and quickly rifled through the drawers.

Frank picked up a bottle of pills with Coach Whiteside's name on it from a bottom drawer. If these were Whiteside's, what was Brundige doing with them? Frank carefully opened the bottle and shook a few capsules onto the desk. Then he scooped up the capsules and dropped them into his shirt pocket. Taking a pencil from the desk, Frank copied the information from the label onto a piece of paper.

Making sure he left everything where he'd found it, Frank went over to the door and opened it slowly. Joe and Davis were leaning against the wall opposite Brundige's door. Joe gave a quick nod to Frank, and Frank slipped out, closing the door behind him.

"Come, on, guys," Frank said. "Let's get out of here." Joe and Davis followed as Frank led them down the corridor and out of the sports complex.

Once outside, Frank let the other two in on

his find. "I think we ought to get these pills analyzed," Frank said as the three walked to the Hardys' van in the dorm parking lot. "Brundige could have tampered with them in some way."

"Dad might be able to help," Joe suggested. "Doesn't he have a connection at that medical lab over on Temple Street? Hop in. We can call him on the car phone."

While Joe started up the car, Frank dialed Fenton Hardy. Frank explained the situation and then listened.

"But, D-dad," he stuttered into the phone. "Yes, I agree. It does seem to be a simple heart attack, but you've always told us to follow every lead." Frank gave a quick nod in his brother's direction, while Davis leaned forward from the backseat.

"Thanks, Dad," Frank said as he wrote down an address on the notepad the Hardys kept on the dash. "We'll see you there." Frank hung up. "Dad's going to meet us at that lab."

"I know right where this is," Joe said as he read the address. "We'll be there pretty quick."

Ten minutes later Joe pulled the van into a parking lot next to a small brick professional building. "There's Dad."

"Hey, Dad," Frank said.

"Hey yourself," Fenton replied affably. "Good to see you, Davis. How are you?"

"I'm okay," Davis said as he shook Fenton's hand. "I really appreciate your help."

"Glad to assist," Fenton answered. He led the guys into the building and to an office on the second floor. After a few minutes' wait in the reception area, Fenton and the boys were greeted by a man wearing a white lab coat. Fenton explained the situation to him briefly, and Frank handed him the pills.

"It could take a little while to test these," the technician said. "But first let's see what the prescription says."

"Thanks, Bob," Fenton said.

"Never a problem." The lab technician smiled. Looking down at the note Frank handed him, the man's smile faded. "Everything appears in order. It's a prescription for heart medication. One question, though." The technician turned toward Frank. "Did you get all the dates right?"

"Absolutely," Frank said quickly.

"Well then, these pills wouldn't have been any good if taken recently. They have a short efficacy span. After forty-five days the tablets might not work. People taking the medication need to get a fresh supply frequently."

The Hardys, Davis, and Fenton were silent.

"Excuse me for a second, guys. I'll just go run those tests."

As the technician walked out of the room, Frank and Joe shared a knowing glance.

"Dad," Joe said, unable to suppress his excitement, "Brundige could have slipped the coach a useless pill. And if he did, Whiteside's last attack was sure to be fatal."

"Joe, do you know what you're saying?" Fenton asked.

"It could have been murder," Frank interjected. "Premeditated—" Just as Frank was about to finish his sentence, the lab technician returned.

"It's pretty serious," he responded. "The pills are placebos. If you were having heart problems and took one of them, you'd probably die. A placebo wouldn't prevent heart failure."

Chapter

8

"THEY'RE FAKES," Frank murmured, amazed.

"That's right," the technician answered. "With no medicinal value. Listen, Fenton. I've got to get back to work. I hope the info helps."

"It sure does," Fenton said. "Thanks."

"Any time." With a wave, the technician walked back into the lab, leaving the little group alone in the reception area.

As soon as the door closed, Joe said, "Open and shut. Brundige is our man."

"But—" Davis began.

"Just a second," Fenton interrupted. He turned to his sons and spoke quickly. "I've got an appointment to keep, but I want you guys to proceed carefully. I'm not even sure about *letting* you stay on this case. You've got an interesting piece of evidence, but you can't exactly tell the authorities you broke into someone's office to obtain it. And it doesn't prove anything. Whiteside could have left those pills in Brundige's office and Brundige just popped them into his desk for safekeeping. You'll need more proof." Fenton sighed and shook his head. "Which means, I suppose, that you ought to continue investigating."

"Don't worry, Dad," Joe said as he, Frank, and Davis followed Fenton out the door and into the parking lot. "We'll be careful."

In the parking lot Fenton opened his car door, then said over his shoulder, "Gee, Joe, I wonder why that doesn't make me feel more secure."

Waving to him as he drove off, Frank and Joe smiled at each other.

"So the case is ours," Joe said to his brother. "Let's get on it."

An hour later Frank, Joe, and a still-stunned Davis were back at the university where they had all been invited to play some ball. Davis couldn't be convinced by Joe that Brundige had anything to do with Whiteside's death and wanted to get his mind off the investigating for a while.

Frank had done his best not to jump to conclusions, knowing that the placebos might have been planted in Brundige's desk. He had pointed out that none of them had any idea why Brundige might have wanted Whiteside dead. Davis was still concerned as the three of them walked toward a small basketball court at the opposite end of campus from the main sports complex.

Reaching the small gym, the guys tossed their coats and gym bags down on the sidelines of the court. A game was in progress as Davis, Frank, and Joe ran through a stretching routine. Frank remembered that Brundige had called this gym the Pit, saying it always saw the hardest action. Lots of players who weren't on the college team played there.

Davis kept stretching while Frank and Joe joined the game, which was something of a free-for-all. Every time Joe went up for a rebound, there was an elbow in his ribs. After every basket, the player who scored yelled at his opponent, getting right in his face.

"These players sure don't like one another," Joe said to Davis as he caught his breath on the sidelines.

"You mean the trash-talking?" Davis laughed. "That goes on all the time. You score a hoop and you got to let your man know that you've beaten him. The kids are just doing it like the pros. Most of the time, they don't mean anything by it, though. It's just a game, right?"

"Somebody forgot to tell these guys that," Joe mumbled.

Just then a player dashed by the guys. Joe watched him run down the court, take a pass in stride, and push around the defender guarding him. Then he slammed the ball through the basket.

"Arrggh! That's game!" the player yelled as he landed. He jogged toward the sideline as his teammates congratulated him. Slapping a high five with one of the players, he made his way toward Davis.

"You want some of that?" he asked, pointing at the hoop. "Or are you just planning to do some ballet?" the player scoffed as Davis continued his stretching routine on the floor. Davis's face remained calm as he slowly lifted his head.

"Our game, is it?" Davis asked. "Okay, guys," he added getting up, "let's play."

Following a pace behind Davis as they stepped on the court, Frank and Joe glanced around. "Davis is pretty cool when it comes to hoops," Joe whispered.

"He's awesome." Frank nodded. "Nothing fazes him."

After the guys picked up two other players to run with them, the game began. The opposing team, the winners of the last game, brought the ball upcourt. Frank guarded the point guard, and Joe, the shooting guard. Davis matched up with the player who had taunted him. Dribbling the ball in front of Frank, the point guard faked a shot and passed the ball to Davis's man, who spun around Davis and laid the ball in the basket.

"Is that all the defense you're gonna play?" the guy asked scornfully as he and Davis trotted downcourt.

Davis ignored him as he fought the other players for offensive position underneath his team's basket. Frank dribbled the ball up and passed it into Davis. Using a spin move of his own, Davis dribbled once and jumped toward the basket. As he released his shot, the defender leaped with him and blocked the ball out-of-bounds.

"Face it, man," Davis's opponent taunted. "You just can't compete at this level. The Pit is only for *real* players. So why don't you take your high school game and go back where you came from?"

"Yeah," another player chimed in.

Close enough to hear the taunts, Frank and

Joe exchanged troubled glances. Davis ignored them and kept on.

The opposing team built a quick lead. But then Davis took over. With his team trailing 5–0, he stole the ball from his loud-mouthed antagonist, raced upcourt, and jammed the ball in the basket. The dunk seemed to wake up the rest of the team. With Davis blocking shots, grabbing rebounds, and scoring at will, they soon evened the score. Finally Frank lofted a perfect alley-oop pass to Davis, who slammed it down for the winning point.

As Davis landed, the tough guy guarding him pushed him to the floor.

"What are you doing, man?" Davis shouted as he scrambled to his feet. "You undercut me!"

"Want to make something of it?" the player yelled back.

Suddenly the other members of the opposing team ran up and surrounded Davis. One of them, the point guard, shoved Davis in the chest. Davis staggered backward and was quickly pinned against the wall of the gym.

"Don't mess with us in the Pit," one of them said, waving a threatening fist at Davis.

"Get out of my face!" Davis shouted back.

"You want to fight?" the trash-talking player said to Davis. He cocked a fist and got ready to swing. "Hold him, fellas! I'm going to teach this guy a lesson!"

"Five against one isn't very fair," Joe shouted as he burst through the players around Davis. With a leap and a flying tackle, Joe knocked a big guy to the ground. Stepping in right behind his brother, Frank stood shoulder to shoulder with Davis.

"Back off," Frank yelled. "We beat you— now get over it."

As Frank spoke, Joe, who had wound up on top of his opponent, jumped to his feet. He, too, stood next to Davis. The other guy scrambled up as well, his face contorted in anger.

"You little—" Joe's opponent said through gritted teeth. "I'll—"

"You'll do nothing," a voice shouted from behind the group. Frank spun around to see a gym monitor approaching. "Break it up before I have you all barred from the Pit." Turning to Frank, Joe, and Davis, the monitor said, "You're new around here, so I suggest you get out fast."

"Thanks," Davis said to the monitor. He was glaring at his antagonists as he, Frank, and Joe grabbed their gear and left.

It was late afternoon and the three of them walked outside into the cold, overcast day.

As Frank, Joe, and Davis stepped onto a path that led back to the middle of campus, Frank blew out a plume of white breath. "So much for some friendly hoops," he said. "What was their prob—"

He was cut off by the sound of running feet behind him. Frank turned and stopped short in surprise.

The players from the gym had followed them. And now five of them stood just inches from Frank's face.

Chapter

9

FRANK TENSED, noticing Joe and Davis doing the same. The tall, broad-shouldered, trash-talking player pushed toward Davis.

"I've got a message for you," he said directly into Davis's face. "If you sign with Bayport, someone's going to break your leg."

"Yeah," one of the other guys said, "Turbo's going to—"

"Quiet!" Davis's opponent cut off his friend. "Your mouth's going to get you in trouble." With a final menacing glare at Davis, the tall guy turned and walked away, his buddies following.

"Why don't you just—" Joe began.

Frank held him back. "Let it go, Joe."

"Yeah," Davis seconded. "Don't sweat it. Those guys don't bother me."

To Frank's ear, Davis didn't sound that convincing. "Just some more dumb talk, huh, Davis?" Frank said lightly. He, Joe, and Davis continued down the walkway.

"Are you kidding?" Joe interrupted. "This is serious. It might even be tied in with—"

Frank threw his brother a glare that told him to be careful about what he said to Davis. Neither of them wanted to upset him or influence his decision about which school to choose.

When they got back to their suite, Joe closed the door and said, "It sure looks like someone wants us off this case." He looked at Davis and Frank, who had collapsed on the sofa.

"I'd have to agree with you there," Frank said. "Too many things have happened to make this all too coincidental." Frank moved off the sofa and sat on the floor, his legs in front of him. He leaned forward to grab his ankles. He closed his eyes and held his stretch for a good thirty seconds. "I wonder," he said half to himself, "if what just happened is connected to Whiteside's death."

Suddenly he sat up straight. "Guys, let's rehash what's gone on since we found Whiteside's body. Maybe there's something we've overlooked."

Davis frowned. He was sprawled out on the

sofa, staring at the ceiling. "I just can't concentrate right now."

"Wait a minute," Joe said. "The more I think about it, the more convinced I am that I saw someone when that door opened and shut in the corridor of the basketball office."

"Yeah?" Frank said. "Maybe Brundige was hiding in the office when we showed up? Maybe he'd been with the coach when his heart acted up and—"

"Gave him a fake pill," Joe and Davis said in unison.

"It could be," Frank said. "And he wasn't there at first while Davis was playing that night." Scooting back so he was leaning against the sofa, Frank shook his head from side to side. "But everything we've got against Brundige is circumstantial. Just about anyone in the basketball program could have been there. And lots of people had to have known about the coach's heart condition. It could even be the other assistant coach, Eddie Zabella. We just don't have enough info to pin this on anyone yet."

"And what about the hoopsters who tried to rough us up," Joe asked as he peeled off his sweatshirt and tossed it into his bedroom. "Where do they fit in?"

"Hmm," Frank muttered. "Didn't one of the guys mention Turbo's name? He could be involved."

"But not with Brundige," Joe reminded his brother. "The two barely speak—which would make it hard to plot a murder."

"Turbo's probably just worried that I'll take his spot in the lineup if I come to Bayport," Davis offered.

"Let's approach this from a different angle," Frank suggested. "Who had a motive?"

"If you mean who might have profited from Whiteside's death," Joe answered, "Brundige, Zabella, Turbo, and even the Packard coach, Pete Trevanian."

"Trevanian?" Davis asked.

"Think about it," Joe answered. "With the Bayport program in turmoil, Packard would have a better chance of landing new recruits. Don't forget what happened at the last game, too."

"Right. And he was pretty weird when he talked with Davis," Frank said, getting up from the floor and pacing back and forth. "We ought to check him out. I think a trip back to Packard is in order."

"Can it wait until morning," Joe asked. "I'm zonked. I need something to eat and then straight to bed."

"Okay," Frank said, and followed Joe into the bedroom they were sharing to change. At the doorway he winked at Davis and slapped his brother on the back. "Hoops are tough. I feel real sorry for you."

"So what about Trevanian," Joe asked Frank and Davis as they sat in the student union cafeteria the next morning. "Do we just head up to Packard and snoop around?"

"I've got to stay here for a noon gathering," Davis said. He was picking at the last of his scrambled eggs. "Then, I've got a three o'clock meeting with an academic advisor. Brundige is going with me. So I'll have to leave the detective work to you guys."

"Be careful on your own," Frank said to his friend. "We'll try to meet up with you before your three o'clock meeting."

Frank turned to his brother. "Before we head back to Packard I want to check something out." Frank pointed to the glossy Packard program guide he'd carried with him from the dorm. "This gave me an idea. It says that Trevanian coached at a number of schools before Packard. Maybe there's something in his past that might link him to Whiteside."

"Could be," Joe answered. He took a last gulp of orange juice and got up from the table. "Let's hit the library. There could be some info on him—a newspaper article or something."

"Exactly what I was thinking," Frank said as he and Davis stood and followed Joe out of the cafeteria. The large, attractive, sky-lighted library was only minutes away. Frank sat down at a computer terminal while Joe and Davis stood on either side of him.

"Let's see what this program has to offer," Frank said as he scanned the page with Trevanian's bio. "Hmm."

"What is it, Frank?" Davis asked.

"This name here." Frank pointed to a line in the bio. "It says Trevanian once coached at Endicott Junior College in a small town in Nebraska. I could've sworn that Endicott was the name Whiteside shouted at Trevanian. Remember? At the game. And right after that, Trevanian stopped accusing Whiteside. Let me just play a hunch." Frank typed in the names Trevanian and Endicott. "These CD-ROM computers are great—they've got so much info. And their cross-referencing capabilities are amazing."

"Look!" Joe said as he stared intently at the monitor. "The computer's found a match."

Frank punched a key and an article appeared from a national sports magazine. It was dated ten years earlier.

Endicott Junior College today acknowledged that two of its players have been dropped from the team for violating school academic standards. Apparently, they received passing grades they did not deserve.

The school is investigating the athletic program, but preliminary reports place no blame on the Endicott coaching staff.

"This could be something," Frank said. "But it doesn't give us much."

"Hang on just a sec," Joe responded. He walked over to the information desk as Frank and Davis waited at the computer. In a minute Joe was back followed by a librarian.

"We're trying to access some small newspapers in Nebraska," Joe told the librarian.

"Well," she answered, "you'll have to get on the Internet and tap into one of the networks that serve that state. Maybe one of the schools, like the university. Let me show you."

Frank pushed the computer keyboard toward the librarian. She tapped a few keys. "There. That server has access to the archives of several Nebraska newspapers."

"Thanks," Joe said as the librarian headed back to her station. He and Davis again looked over Frank's shoulder as he typed Trevanian and Endicott into the computer.

"Pay dirt," Frank said excitedly, then began reading aloud from an article in a small Nebraska daily.

Sources claim that Coach Trevanian took money to push his players to transfer to particular four-year schools. Unconfirmed reports indicate that Trevanian also pressured instructors at Endicott to give his players passing grades for classes they rarely attended. A press release issued from the college president's office acknowledged that Trevanian has resigned. But on advice from legal counsel, the president refused any further comment.

"This certainly complicates things," Frank said. "If Whiteside exposed this, Trevanian might have lost his job at Packard. It could be a strong motive for murder."

Joe clapped his brother on the shoulder. "Let's head back to Packard to see what else we can dig up!"

"What's the plan when we get to campus?" Joe asked his brother from behind the wheel of the van. Frank and Joe had left Davis back in Bayport and were now about five minutes away from Packard.

"I'm counting on Trevanian having already left to come down to Bayport for the big rematch tomorrow," Frank answered. "If he's gone, we might be able to get in and search his office."

When they reached the Packard campus, Joe pulled the van into the gym parking lot. The

Hardys made their way to the entrance and walked nonchalantly through the complex to Trevanian's office. It was in the corner and well away from most foot traffic.

Listening for any noise in the office, Frank cautiously tried the doorknob. It was locked. He jimmied it open quickly, and he and Joe entered the office to begin their search. Quietly shuffling through papers, the Hardys found nothing to link Trevanian to any of the recent events.

"Shhh!" Frank put an index finger to his lips. "Do you hear that?"

Footsteps sounded in the hall, and they were growing louder. The Hardys froze in place, both staring at the office door. There was no place to hide. The footsteps had stopped right in front of the door as the silhouette of a man appeared, framed in the door's opaque glass windowpane.

"Great!" the Hardys heard someone mutter.

It was Coach Trevanian.

"What did I do with my keys?"

Frank and Joe were trapped. Then Frank glanced at the desk. There on the edge was a set of keys.

"Joe," Frank whispered, "his keys," he said, pointing to the desk. "He can't get in." The footsteps moved away as Trevanian's silhouette disappeared.

"He must be going to get someone to open the door for him," Frank reasoned in a hushed voice.

"Quick, before he comes back," Joe said as he sprinted to the door. He opened it slowly. When he saw Trevanian turn the corner of the corridor, he signaled his brother to follow. "Let's get out of here."

Back in the van, Frank stuck the key in the ignition.

"That was pretty much a waste of time," Joe said in frustration. Just then a voice startled him. It was Coach Trevanian. He was standing right next to Joe's window.

"What are you guys doing here?" the coach asked. "Where's Davis? I thought he was scheduled to be touring the Bayport campus."

"We, I—I mean we wanted to check out a few things about Packard for ourselves," Frank answered hesitantly. "We have to pick colleges soon, too, so—"

Joe shot a worried glance at his brother. Maybe Trevanian knew they'd been in his office checking him out.

Trevanian only dismissed them with a cold sneer. "Whatever," the coach said, walking away.

Joe sighed audibly. "I don't think he knew we were in his office." He relaxed into the pas-

84

senger seat as Frank put the blinker on and pulled out.

"I agree," Frank said. "Though I do think he's a bit suspicious of us."

Just as Frank was steering the van through a sharp curve on the highway a dark sedan pulled out seemingly from nowhere and passed them on the right. As it shot ahead of the van, it swerved left into Frank's lane, forcing Frank to yank the wheel left and hit the brake.

"What—" Frank shouted. He pressed hard on his horn as he tried to maintain control of the van. The car sped past and again swerved into the van's path. "Hold on!" Frank said. They were rounding another curve, and it was all Frank could do to keep them from skidding out of control. The van's left tires squealed through the loose dirt along the median.

"I can't get any traction to brake!" Frank shouted as he felt the back of the van fishtail. "We're going to spin out!"

But with a quick yank on the wheel, Frank was able to get the van back on the road and straightened out.

"Here he comes again!" Joe yelled to Frank. "Watch it!"

The car swerved at them, and this time Frank had to jerk the wheel to the left with all his force.

"Look out, Frank!" Joe shouted as he braced his hands on the dashboard.

Before Joe could finish his sentence, Frank saw what Joe was talking about. Frank had swerved into oncoming traffic—right into the path of an eighteen-wheeler!

Chapter

10

"FRAAA-NNK!" JOE SHOUTED. "That semi is coming right at us!"

With his hands gripped tightly to the steering wheel, Frank tried to regain control of the van. The semi was bearing down hard on them, its lights flashing and air horn blaring. The black sedan was still beside the van on the right, blocking Frank's way. The only thing to do was to swerve even farther left and hope that no car or truck was in the lane beside the semi.

"Hang on!" Frank said through gritted teeth.

Just as the semi was about to smash into them, Frank pulled the car sharply to the left. Tires squealing, the van skidded across the second lane of oncoming traffic and onto the dirt service road beside the highway. Kicking up a cloud of dust, the van screeched to a halt inches from a utility pole.

"Whew!" Joe let out a long breath as he slumped back in his seat. "That was close."

"Too close," Frank agreed. He released his death grip on the steering wheel and turned to see if the dark sedan was anywhere in sight. It had disappeared. "You okay, Joe?" he finally asked.

"No," Joe said sternly. He banged his fist on the dashboard. "Now it's getting personal. That car deliberately tried to run us into the truck!"

"Maybe Trevanian followed us from Packard," Frank said. "Or Brundige trailed us from Bayport. You didn't happen to recognize anyone in the sedan?"

"Nope," Joe answered curtly. "It had tinted windows."

"We'll just have to step up our investigation," Frank said. "Meanwhile, it still makes sense to keep this quiet. We need to get some hard evidence. If we confronted Brundige or Trevanian now, this thing could blow up in our faces."

Frank turned the car around on the service road and followed it back toward Packard. Reaching an exit where he could make a U-turn, Frank headed back toward Bayport. The rest of the ride was silent as the two boys pondered their second close call in as many days.

Seeing the highway turnoff to campus, Frank exited, then pulled into a drive-through burger joint. "Six cheeseburgers, three large fries, and three large root beers," Frank said at the window. "I figure we'll take something back for Davis," he explained to his brother. "And if he's not around, I'm sure you'll be able to force his down."

"How about a burger?" Joe asked as he opened the door to their suite and saw Davis sitting on the sofa.

"Sounds great." Davis smiled. "That alumni meeting had only cheese and crackers." Davis took the delectable-smelling bag Joe held out to him. "Anything come of your trip to Packard?" he asked between bites of his first burger.

"Nothing," Frank said, speaking around a mouth full of fries. "Unless you count being almost flattened by a semi."

"What?" Davis exclaimed.

"Somebody didn't want us to return from Packard alive," Joe answered from his windowsill perch. "And I think it's just a little too coincidental that Trevanian saw us in our van just minutes before we were run off the road."

"I'm not convinced," Frank countered. "Brundige could have followed us—"

"Hey, guys," Davis interrupted, wiping his mouth with a paper napkin. "I'd love to hear

89

what you're thinking, but I've got that three o'clock meeting with Brundige and the academic advisor." Davis got up, tossed his burger wrappers in the trash, and headed for the door. "You feel like tagging along?"

"Probably a good idea," Frank agreed.

"Come on then," Davis said as he led the way. "Brundige said he'd meet me here and walk me back over to the gym."

"Isn't that Brundige?" Joe said, pointing through some evergreen shrubs that lined the front walkway. The man Joe was pointing to was standing at a side door of the dorm. "He seems to be having an argument with someone."

"That looks like Turbo Thomson," Davis whispered.

The Hardys and Davis paused to listen, taking cover behind the shrubs.

"Where have you been? You've been gone all day," they overheard Brundige say.

"It's none of your business, man!" Turbo snarled.

The two stood facing each other with dark scowls on their faces. From behind the bushes, the three saw Brundige check his watch.

"Listen, I'm expecting someone," Brundige told Turbo. "We'll settle this later. Just be ready for the next practice, will you!"

Without answering Brundige, Turbo stormed

90

past him and stalked into the dorm through the side entrance.

"Let's go meet him," Frank said quietly. He led Davis and Joe around the bushes.

"Here he is, Davis," Frank said in a loud, nonchalant voice. They stepped onto the side path where Brundige stood. "Hi, Coach."

Hearing Frank, Brundige turned around.

"Nice to see you, fellas," Brundige answered in a distracted tone.

"I'm ready to meet with the academic counselor," Davis said with a slightly forced smile. "I want to find out about premed—"

"That's fine," Brundige said curtly. "Listen, can we make this quick? I've got some things to take care of. The academic advisor who works with athletes has her office in the athletic complex. Follow me."

Brundige walked ahead of Davis and the Hardys and was silent all the way.

"Real friendly, huh? Was it something we said?" Joe whispered to Frank as the four of them entered the office of the academic advisor, located directly above the coaches' corridor.

"I doubt it. Most likely it's because he didn't make head coach," Frank answered in a hushed voice.

"Or because he's a murderer."

"Tone it down, Joe," Frank chastised his

91

brother quietly. "I'm suspicious, too, but we need proof."

After being introduced to the advisor, Frank and Joe sat by silently as she told Davis about the programs the athletic department could offer, like extra tutoring and study halls. Throughout the meeting, Brundige said nothing. He stared out the window, tapping his fingers on the sides of his chair.

Frank found his mind wandering to Brundige's confrontation with Turbo. The guys who'd threatened Davis outside the Pit had mentioned Turbo. Despite appearances, *could* there be a connection between the player and the assistant coach? Frank wondered.

"Thanks for your time," Frank heard Davis say, rousing him from his speculations. "I appreciate the help," Davis went on as he rose from his seat.

"Okay, then," Brundige said getting up, too. "That should answer your questions, Davis. Now I've got to get going." Brundige practically pushed the guys out of the advisor's office. "You know the way back to the dorm," he suggested almost antagonistically. When Davis nodded yes, Brundige was gone in a flash, leaving the boys alone and befuddled.

"Not quite the welcome I imagined." Davis laughed lightly. "Between Packard's Coach Trevanian and Brundige, my choices don't seem all that great anymore." Frank and Joe both could hear the disappointment in his voice.

Leaving the athletic complex, the guys crossed the main quadrangle. Following Davis's lead, Frank and Joe remained silent. Once inside the dorm suite, Davis paced the living room. After a few minutes he headed to the door.

"I've got to get some air, guys," he announced. "Clear my head a little." Just then a noise at the door caught everyone's attention.

"Look," Joe said quickly.

An envelope had been slid under the door and now lay on the carpet. To Joe it looked out of place and vaguely malevolent.

Davis sucked in his breath sharply and then said, "Great. More bad news."

Chapter

11

SPEEDING TO THE DOOR, Joe opened it and peered outside. Nobody was there. "Whoever left the note sure was fast," Joe announced as he turned back.

Davis and Frank were both standing in the center of the room. Davis had picked up the letter and was reading it.

"What does it say?" Joe asked.

Davis stared blankly at the page. Finishing the letter, he handed it to Frank and walked over to the window.

"What does it say?" Joe repeated.

"Go ahead," Davis said to Frank.

Quietly, but with a firm voice, Frank read the note. " 'Don't double-cross us. If you don't play for Bayport, you won't play for anyone. Remember, the CBA doesn't take kindly to players on the take.'"

"But you're not on the take!" Joe exclaimed. "Nobody would believe that."

"I don't know," Davis answered, pacing. Frank could see how worried his friend was. "College hoops is full of scandal—players taking money for no-show jobs, getting free cars and clothes from boosters. It happens all the time. And once you're tainted, it's hard to convince people you're not on the take."

"That's not fair," Joe said.

"Fair or not, that's the way it works," Davis answered. "That's why I wanted to choose a clean program. I thought Bayport or Packard fit the bill. I guess I was wrong. Now it looks like my college career will be over before it starts."

"Don't think that way," Frank implored his friend.

"No, Frank," Davis said with a frown, "whoever wrote this note is right. The College Basketball Association won't stand for even a hint of impropriety. I think I'm in real trouble."

Frank, who was still holding the note, walked over to his friend. "I don't want to sound like an alarmist, but I think the bribe money is the least of our worries," he said. "You've got people wanting to harm you if you come to Bayport or if you don't."

"I know, Frank," Davis said. "I remember what Turbo's buddies said." Davis managed a weak smile as he wandered over to the window and stared out. "Guys," he continued after a minute, "let's get some dinner. I need to clear my head. All this is too confusing—and dangerous," he added softly.

"Now, that's a good idea," Joe said. "A strategy session and dinner—the perfect combo. How about it, Frank?"

"I'm already there," Frank said as he ushered Davis and Joe toward the door.

A few minutes later the guys were seated in the student union cafeteria, their plates piled high with the dinner special—fried chicken.

"Let's take another look at that letter," Joe said as he took a bite from a drumstick. He was sitting across from Frank and Davis. "Does it say anything else that might clue us in on who's harassing Davis and who might have murdered Whiteside?"

"Well," Frank answered, "it implies that since Davis has said nothing about the money, it must mean that he's accepting the offer to play for Bayport. Then it makes the threat about not double-crossing them. And it's signed 'The New Head Coach.'"

"Zabella," Joe said solemnly.

"Could be," Davis commented. "But I'm not sure a coach would do this. It doesn't make sense that Zabella would just send money without talking to a player, feeling him out first. You know, hinting around that money was available."

"I agree," Frank said. "Whoever sent the money took a big chance that Davis wouldn't immediately alert the police or the CBA."

"Besides," Davis added as he picked up an onion ring, "wouldn't Zabella try to calm things down around here now that he's the interim head coach?"

"Actually, anyone could have sent the money," Joe admitted as he watched students move through the cafeteria.

"The amateurish way it was handled makes me think that someone could have been setting up the Bayport program," Frank suggested. "Maybe the sender *wanted* Davis to go public with the bribe and opt to go to another college. Bad publicity would taint Bayport's program and send good recruits to its rivals."

"Like Packard," Davis and Joe said simultaneously.

"Exactly," Frank agreed. "And that makes Coach Trevanian a real suspect. At least, in terms of the bribe and threats."

"So you don't think he murdered Whiteside?" Davis asked.

"I suppose he could have. He sure didn't like

him. Plus he had something to hide that White-side knew about," Frank replied.

"You mean what happened back at Endi-cott," Joe said.

Davis nodded. "Right. I'd almost forgotten about that."

"It's almost as if we have two cases going at once—Whiteside's death and the bribe," Frank said speculatively.

"Three cases," Joe corrected his brother. "Don't forget about the guys at the pick-up game who told Davis *not* to attend Bayport. They mentioned Turbo. Maybe he got his buddies to go after Davis because he's worried Davis'll take his spot on the team."

"You're right, Joe," Frank said. "Three cases and at least as many suspects."

"So what do we do now?" Davis asked.

Joe swallowed the last bit of his chicken. "Back to the dorm for a good sleep," he said, getting up from his seat. "And tomorrow we look for some answers."

Davis and the Hardys walked quickly back to the dorm through the brisk night air. Racing up the stairs to warm themselves, they were back in their room in no time. Davis hit the bathroom, while Frank and Joe donned pajamas.

"Good night, fellas," Davis said as he came out. "I'll see you in the morning."

" 'Night, Davis," Frank and Joe responded.

"We'll hit the sack, too," Frank added, turning off the lights and following Joe into their room.

"I didn't realize I was so tired." Joe yawned as the Hardys climbed into their bunks. "I don't think anything could get me out of bed," he said as he pulled the covers over him. In a few minutes both brothers were fast asleep.

"Ehh! Urrggh!" Joe coughed, rousing himself from sleep. "What—" he said as he sat up in bed. He coughed again as he realized he was surrounded by smoke. "Frank!" he shouted.

"What?" Frank said groggily.

"It's a fire. Come on!" Joe yelled as he jumped out of bed. Smoke was coming in from under the door. Frank, too, was up in a flash.

"Try the door with this," he said as he pushed a towel into his brother's hands. "See if the handle's hot. We've got to get to Davis."

Joe touched the door panel lightly. "Not too bad. I don't think the fire's directly behind the door." He turned the handle, pushed the door open, and sprinted out, with Frank following close behind. The living room was filled with suffocating smoke and a blazing fire.

"On your knees, Joe," Frank shouted. "The air's better down there." Frank turned toward his friend's door. It was open. "Davis!" he yelled.

"Here, guys!" Davis shouted back. Frank and

99

Joe could barely make out Davis beyond the flames that were engulfing the couch. He was pounding on the door that led into the hall. "Help!" he screamed in a panicked voice. "It's jammed."

"Down on your knees, Davis," Frank yelled. "Crawl on the floor. I'm going to try the window."

Frank moved around his brother, who was trying to smother part of the fire on the couch with a towel in his hands. Reaching the window, Frank stood up and yanked at the frame. It didn't budge. Straining with all his might, Frank pulled harder. The frame still didn't move.

"Guys!" he yelled. "Give me a hand. The window's stuck."

Joe and Davis crawled over to his side. The three put their hands on the window and pushed hard, but it remained shut tight. Frank, Joe, and Davis stared in horror.

"It's no use," Frank said. "We're trapped!"

Chapter

12

Squinting through the smoke, Frank scanned the living room. He grabbed a heavy wooden desk chair and shouted to Davis and Joe to grab the mattresses off the beds.

With a loud crash, Frank shattered the window. Smoke and fire leaped toward the opening.

"Quick!" Frank said. "Drop the mattresses out the window to break our fall. It's only about fifteen feet to the ground."

After kicking out a few large shards of glass that remained stuck to the frame, Frank placed a blanket on the sill.

"Joe!" Frank said, coughing. He pointed to the window. "Go first, then spot for Davis. And remember, jump and roll!"

"Right," Joe said as he lifted himself up onto the sill. With a quick look back at his brother and Davis, Joe leaped. Landing lightly, he somersaulted off the mattresses and scrambled to his knees.

Davis was next. Bending his lanky body, he crouched on the sill. "I'm coming, Joe," he shouted as he pushed off. Davis landed softly, his athletic frame easily absorbing the shock of the fall. Joe gave him a hand up. He and Davis looked up at the window. There, they saw Frank poised on the sill, silhouetted against the leaping flames.

"Hurry," Joe shouted. "We've got you covered."

Frank nodded and jumped from the window. Hitting the mattresses, Frank curled and rolled, then felt his brother and Davis grab him.

"We made it," Frank said as the two helped him to his feet. Davis and Joe nodded in agreement. Staring up at the fire, the three of them were silent for a moment, stunned by the realization of how close they had come to dying.

Sirens shook the guys from their reverie. Alarm bells were going off inside the dorm as well, and a number of students were streaming out of the dorm. As the fire trucks reached the scene, the resident assistant came up to the guys.

"You okay?" he asked as firefighters rushed

past them and directed a fire hose at the flaming window. "Let's get you over to the paramedics." The assistant herded the guys over to an EMS truck. After a check of their vital signs, the paramedic gave them a clean bill of health.

"The fire's been put out," the resident assistant told the guys as they were thanking the EMS workers. "Evidently the fire was confined to your living room. It didn't even spread into the bedrooms, so your gear is okay. Come with me," the RA added. "I'll put you in another suite so you can rest."

Walking into the dorm through the back entrance, Frank was startled to see Coach Trevanian strolling in ahead of them. He was surrounded by some of his players.

"Coach Trevanian," Frank shouted as he ran to catch up with the coach. Joe and Davis followed.

The coach turned around at the sound of his name. The four stood in the back lobby of the dorm.

"Oh, hi," he said. "Frank, is it? And Davis and Joe," the coach added. "You fellas weren't involved in that fire, were you?"

"Unfortunately, yes," Davis answered.

"Well, I'm sure glad you weren't hurt," the coach said, smiling. He faced Davis. "Other than this fire, how's your visit to Bayport been?"

103

"Not bad," Davis responded noncommittally.

"Coach," Frank interjected with a hint of skepticism in his voice, "what's your team doing at the Bayport dorm? Do you always stay on the opposing team's campus for a ballgame?"

"Not usually," Trevanian said. "But Bayport's got this new athletic dorm and offered to put us up. We've been around since this afternoon. The big game is tomorrow night, you know."

Trevanian turned back toward Davis. "Stop by our practice in the morning, son," he said. "It might help you decide to become a Wildcat. And if you want to chat, I'm staying in Suite 109 just down the hall here." Trevanian pointed toward the east corridor. "Well, take it easy then, guys," he added. "I'm sure glad you're okay."

"Appreciate it, Coach," Davis said as Trevanian walked down the hall to his suite.

"Well, that was interesting," Joe said when the Packard coach was out of earshot. "If Trevanian's been here that long, he could have set the fire."

"Just what I was thinking," Frank agreed.

Just then the resident assistant walked up to the guys. "Here, fellas," he said, handing some keys to Davis and Joe. "I got you a suite here on the first floor. It's Number 105. I had your bags moved. I also got a call from campus security. They'd like to talk to you in the morning. By that time, the fire marshal should have some info for us." The resident assistant smiled. "And if there's anything I can do, just let me know."

"Thanks," the guys said in unison.

"For now, we'll just get some sleep," Frank added as they headed down the hall. "It's been quite a night!"

"That's all I can tell you, fellas."

Davis and the Hardys were sitting in the office of the school security chief. After a breakfast of cereal and fruit at the cafeteria, they'd gone over to the administration building for a ten o'clock meeting.

"The fire marshal is a bit suspicious, but he's got no evidence of foul play," the security official continued as he looked out the window of his third-story office overlooking the main quad. "So he asked me to question you about what happened. Did you see or smell anything strange before the flames broke out? Could it have been an electrical fire?"

"We were asleep," Frank said, trying hard to keep his temper in check. "Look, sir," he continued. "That suite was a firebox. The fire marshal must have found out something by now."

"Nothing definite as yet," the security chief responded. "These investigations take time."

"Nothing definite," Joe blurted out angrily.

He leaned forward in his chair and scowled. "Our room was practically sealed shut and the window jammed! What more proof does he need?" Frank and Davis nodded in agreement.

"Okay, guys," the official responded in a quiet voice. Frank saw beads of sweat form on the man's brow. "Let me level with you. With all the construction and renovation going on around campus, it's been hard for us to keep up with everything. But we'll get on it now." The man rose from his chair.

"But, we nearly di—" Joe began.

"It's all right, sir," Frank said, interrupting his brother. "For now, we'll leave it at that. But we are going to want some answers soon." Frank shepherded an incredulous Joe and Davis out of the security official's office.

"Thanks for your cooperation," the official said as they left.

Once outside the administration building, Joe lit into his brother. "Why did you let him off the hook so easily?"

"I wanted to buy us some more time," Frank said. He, Davis, and Joe were heading across campus to the athletic complex. "Once the fire marshal decides it was arson, everything will blow sky high. But until he does, the case is ours alone. For now, we don't want to scare off our suspects. Remember, we need hard proof."

"I get it," Joe admitted. "Still, that guy's attitude makes me mad."

"Me, too," Davis seconded. "I'm tired of getting the runaround from everyone."

"I know, guys," Frank agreed, patting his friend on the shoulder. "But despite the danger, the fewer people on the case, the better. And when we need them, I'll be the first to call in the cavalry."

"What's this?" Davis wondered aloud as they approached the athletic complex. They were following a walkway from the administration building, but their path was blocked by a detour sign. Davis ran a hand along a barricade of yellow tape surrounding a couple of small buildings near the sports construction site. Peering beyond it, the guys saw a number of construction workers gathered around a line of trailers on the far edge of the site.

"They're going to do some blasting," Frank answered, pointing to a sign posted on the fence that said: DANGER. BLASTING UNDER WAY. STAY BEHIND BARRICADES. LISTEN FOR SIRENS AND FOLLOW INSTRUCTIONS.

"They're demolishing those old buildings near the arena," Frank said. "Remember, we saw them when Brundige was telling us about the new sports complex."

As Frank spoke, a loudspeaker blared.

"Warning! Warning! Five minutes to blasting. Please stay behind the yellow markers."

"This ought to be a good show," Joe said. "I've always thought I'd make a good demolition man," he said, laughing. "Let's check it out."

Making sure to stay behind the barriers, Davis and the Hardys found a good spot at the corner of the demolition area. A small crowd of onlookers had gathered across the taped-off site from them. The speaker system blared again. "Two minutes to blasting. Warning! Warning!"

Glancing over at the row of trailers, Frank saw a figure sneak out of the one at the far end of the row.

"Hey! Isn't that Turbo?" he said, nudging his brother.

"Where?" Joe asked.

"Over by that trailer. Look. Now he's running toward the buildings that are going to be demolished." For a second the Hardys lost sight of Turbo, their vision blocked by the trailers.

"Thirty seconds to blasting. Warning! Warning! All clear. Counting down from thirty ... twenty-nine ... twenty-eight ..."

The Hardys and Davis turned and saw Turbo running between two buildings.

"Oh, no," Frank gasped. "He's fallen."

"Twenty-one ... twenty ... nineteen ..."

"He's not getting up! If those buildings blow,

he's sure to be crushed!" Davis shouted in horror. Bursting past his brother and Davis, Joe pushed under the tape and ran toward the fallen basketball player. "I'll get him!" he said. "Try to make them stop the blasting!"

"Joe! Don't! There's not time!" Frank screamed.

"Twelve ... eleven ... ten ..."

"Come on, Davis," Frank said frantically. "We've got to stop the countdown."

The two sprinted around the tape barrier in the direction of the trailers. Rounding the side of the closest trailer, they waved their arms wildly, shouting at the construction workers.

"Five ... four ... three ..."

"Stop!" they both screamed at the top of their lungs, but no one heard them as sirens announced the coming blast.

"Two ... one ... DETONATE!"

Frank and Davis reached the startled workers in time to stare in horror as the buildings came crashing down in a shower of deadly debris.

"Noooo!" Frank screamed.

Chapter

13

"THEY'LL BE BURIED ALIVE," Frank yelled frantically. A cloud of dust enveloped the blast site as Frank ran toward the spot where he had last seen his brother. Squinting, he saw huge mounds of rubble where the buildings had once stood.

Davis followed, sprinting past startled construction workers. The two covered the fifty or so yards in seconds, scrambling over cement rubble and mangled iron.

"Joe!" Frank shouted. "Where are you? Can you hear me?" Frank raced to the mound of debris that had been the first building, pulling boulders and rocks away in a frantic search for his brother. "We've got to get to them!" Frank

screamed to Davis, who had run toward a second rubble pile and was also screaming for Joe.

"I'm here," a faint voice called. It was Joe.
He was slowly climbing out of a small ditch surrounded by piles of cement blocks.

"Joe," Frank said with relief, running to his
brother, "are you all right?"

"I think so," Joe answered. Grabbing his
brother's outstretched hand, Joe pulled himself
out of the ditch. "Lucky for me, this ditch was
here." Joe pointed down toward the hole. "That
sheet metal covered me. But where's Turbo?"
he asked. "Is he dead?"

"I don't know," Frank answered.

As Frank spoke, tires screeched on the road
that ran beside the demolition site.

"Look," Davis shouted. "It's Turbo! In that
black sedan!" The driver's side window was
rolled down. Frank and Joe could see that Davis
was right. It was Turbo, and he was very much
alive.

"What was he doing prowling around the
blast site?" Joe exclaimed. "I mean, I almost
got myself killed trying to save him."

Just then someone shouted at the three guys.
It was the construction site foreman. He and the
rest of the crew had just reached them.

"What do you think you were doing? You
could have been killed."

"I know, sir," Frank said in an apologetic

tone. "My brother here, I mean . . ." He hesitated. "Well, his dog got loose and he ran to save him."

The workers were incredulous.

"Funny thing, though," Frank continued. "The dog ran back to the car."

Joe dusted himself off. "No harm done, I guess."

"Funny thing," the foreman mimicked Frank scornfully. "You might have died. Now get out of here!"

"Right away," the guys agreed. They headed for the arena, leaving the construction workers shaking their heads.

"I think it's about time to confront Turbo," Joe said, continuing to brush dust off his clothes.

Frank nodded. "Let's hit the practice," he suggested. "Maybe we can get more info out of Brundige and Zabella, too."

After a quick stop at a men's room to clean up Joe, the guys installed themselves in courtside seats in the arena. The whole Bayport team was clearly wired about the big game, running drills and shooting—with the exception of Turbo. He was nowhere to be seen. After about forty minutes, Coach Zabella whistled, signaling their practice was over. Brundige stayed behind and walked over to Davis, Frank, and Joe.

"Hey, guys," Brundige said. "How are you?"

He addressed Davis. "The practice went well, don't you think?"

"We didn't see Turbo out there," Frank commented.

"No, you didn't," Brundige answered mechanically. He rolled his eyes ever so slightly and sighed. "I don't know where he is or what we're going to do with him—" Brundige stopped abruptly, a smile appearing on his face. "But you guys shouldn't worry about Turbo. How about a late lunch on me?"

"Sure," Davis answered for the guys, and the threesome got up from their seats.

"Pizza at the student union okay with you?"

With an arm around his shoulder, Brundige led Davis off the court and out of the arena. As the four walked toward the cafeteria, Frank and Joe fell a few paces behind.

"What do you make of Brundige now?" Joe whispered to his brother. "He seems almost too friendly."

Frank nodded. "He's been through a lot. But if he is our man, we might be able to use his friendliness to pump him for info."

"Come on, fellas. Let's eat." Brundige was holding a side door into the union open for the Hardys.

"Sounds great," Joe said, passing through directly into the cafeteria. While Davis and the

Hardys sat down at a booth, Brundige ordered two pies and sodas for the four of them.

When the coach reached the table, he sat down and said, "I want to apologize to you all for my behavior over the past few days. Not being named interim head coach was a blow—especially after all the stuff I had to take as an assistant to Whiteside. He could be a bear, you know. And the athletic director really blind-sided me by choosing Eddie Zabella without even telling me. I was ready to explode."

"I understand," Davis said hesitantly, but he couldn't hide a frown, though. "What are the team's plans for me?"

"If I were the head coach, you'd be starting," Brundige answered. "But I don't know if I'm even going to be around next year. I promise, though, that I'll talk to Eddie. I'm sure he'll want you here."

After a few more minutes a waitress arrived with their pizzas.

"Dig in," Brundige said, handing a plate to Joe, who was sitting next to him.

"You and Zabella don't get along very well, do you?" Frank asked cautiously as he reached for a slice.

Brundige laughed. "No, son," he admitted, leaning back in his seat. "We've never been best friends. Look. I don't want to turn you off to Bayport, Davis. But over the past few years, Zabella really put a wedge between Whiteside and me."

"How?" Davis asked.

"He'd disagree with me when we discussed strategy with Coach W—no matter what I suggested, he'd be opposed to it." Brundige stared out the window at the quad. "Before he came to Bayport," he continued, "I was in line to succeed Whiteside. And now—"

"And now," Joe interjected, "Zabella's the interim head coach."

"That's not even the worst of it," Brundige said. "I got into coaching because I wanted to help kids be the best they could be, get a college degree, you know. You asked about Turbo before. Well, he was a protégé of mine. I recruited him, helped him keep his grades up. But then Whiteside cut his playing time, and Turbo blamed me. He started skipping practices.

"To make matters worse, Zabella befriended him, telling him he'd make him a star. Zabella used Turbo to create dissension on the team."

Brundige was silent for a few moments. "I don't know why I'm playing true confessions with you guys, but—" The coach paused again and looked at his watch. "It's late. I've got to be going. We've got a five o'clock practice and I have to go over strategy with Zabella before then." He got up from the booth. "I'll see you at the game tonight."

"You sure will," Davis said, grabbing another slice of pizza. "Good luck against Packard."

Brundige nodded and left the cafeteria.

"I'll tell you one thing," Frank said once Brundige was out of earshot. "The Zabella-Turbo connection is intriguing. Zabella might have put Turbo up to threatening us. At any rate, it's worth checking out. Maybe, in the meantime, we ought to see what we can find in Trevanian's room."

"The coast is clear," Joe whispered to his brother. "Davis just gave me the sign." He and Frank were hidden in the stairwell next to Coach Trevanian's room. They had instructed Davis to tell them when Trevanian and the Packard team left for their afternoon practice at the gym.

"Okay. Let's go," Frank said quietly. He carefully came out into the hall and approached Trevanian's room. Jimmying the lock, Frank slipped into the dark room with Joe right behind him.

"I'll check the desk," Joe said, stepping around his brother. "You look through his clothes."

Pulling out drawers, Joe found nothing. "Got anything?" he asked Frank, who was standing at the closet. Joe saw that Frank had a piece of paper in his hand.

"Yeah," Frank answered. "Look at this. It's a bank withdrawal slip for ten thousand dollars."

"So it looks like Trevanian was behind the bribe to Davis," Joe reasoned. "He must have wanted Davis to go to the CBA."

"Yeah," Frank said. He put the slip back into the coat pocket where he'd found it. "It sure looks that way. But now it's time to get out of here."

"It's a relief to know that Whiteside wasn't in on the bribe," Davis said when the Hardys told him about their discovery. It was getting close to five o'clock. The Packard-Bayport game was at eight. "But that still leaves a possible murderer on the loose, doesn't it? A murderer who's after *us*, too."

"I'm afraid so," Frank agreed. "I think the only thing to do is keep poking around. We'll watch our backs, but we've got to find some hard evidence."

"And how are we going to do that?" Joe asked.

"Maybe we can check out Zabella's office," Frank answered. "Brundige said they'll be working out in the practice gym at five." He looked at his watch. "It's about that time. If we hurry, we should be able to slip in while they're on the court."

Sprinting from the dorm, across the main

quad, and past the student union, Davis and the Hardys arrived at the sports complex in a matter of minutes. The coaches' corridor was deserted, just as Frank had hoped.

"You're getting good at this," Joe whispered to his brother. Frank had just jimmied open Coach Zabella's office door.

"Practice makes perfect," Frank said. "Now let's get to work. Davis, you go check out practice. If—"

"I know," Davis said. "If Zabella heads back this way, I'll alert you."

Frank managed a smile. "You've got the detective thing down."

"Yep." Davis nodded as he headed toward the gym. Meanwhile, the Hardys stepped into Zabella's office.

Checking out the coach's desk, Frank found little. Joe was checking the bookcase by the window when a large book sticking out from others in the row caught his eye. Joe took the book from the shelf and motioned Frank over to him.

"Look at this," he said quietly. Frank saw that his brother had a *Physician's Desk Reference* in his hands. Joe opened the book to a page marked with a strip of paper. "This could be proof of Zabella's involvement," Joe continued, his voice rising with excitement. "The page on heart medications has been marked."

"Circumstantial, Joe," Frank told his brother.

"We'd need something more incriminating." Frank returned to Zabella's desk and booted up the computer. "Maybe this will help."

Frank and Joe waited impatiently for a few moments before the computer's directory flashed on the screen. Scrolling down through the list, Frank punched up a file titled Head Coach. After a few whirs and clicks, a series of letters appeared on the monitor. Frank and Joe bent over the screen.

"We've got motive," Frank almost cried out as he read from the screen. "Listen to this. 'You better retire and see that I'm named head coach. I'm tired of playing second fiddle. You've made promises and now it's time to keep them—or else!' "

Frank scrolled down the text farther. "Zabella was really ticked that Whiteside kept postponing his promise to step down."

"He must be our man, all right," Joe agreed. Just then the Hardys heard footsteps coming down the corridor. Taking no chances, they shut off the computer and waited. The footsteps stopped in front of the office. Frank and Joe stared at each other tensely. It was Zabella.

"This way." Joe motioned Frank to move over to the inner door that linked Zabella's office to Brundige's. "In here."

Just as Zabella opened his door and stepped in the office, Frank quietly shut the door behind him. Crouching down below the opaque windowpane, the Hardys waited breathlessly. They could hear Zabella walk over to his desk and punch in numbers on the phone.

After a few seconds they heard him mutter angrily, "I've got to get back before they miss me. But you listen up. You're already in this up to your neck whether you like it or not. So get over here and finish the job. I want this problem dealt with. That friend of Davis's saw me, and I want them all dead!"

Chapter
14

FRANK STARED AT JOE, his heart racing. Seconds later he heard Zabella slam down the receiver, the door close, and Zabella's footsteps move down the hall. Frank opened the connecting door a crack and peered into the office.

"All clear," he whispered to his brother.

"So it was Zabella I saw the night Whiteside died," Joe said quietly. "And now, he wants me—no, all of us—dead."

"Come on." Frank motioned his brother quietly. "Let's get out of here and find Davis." Frank closed the door to Zabella's office and then walked to the one that led directly into the corridor. Cracking it a bit, Frank peered down the hall. "Okay."

He and Joe stepped into the hall and headed back to the gymnasium. Turning a corner, they ran smack into a breathless Davis.

"Guys," their friend said with a relieved look on his face, "you're okay! I saw Zabella leave practice and head toward the offices. I figured I'd better warn you."

"Good thinking," Frank said, leading Davis and Joe back to the gym. Then he filled in Davis on what they'd just overheard.

"He's going to kill us?" Davis exclaimed in shock.

Frank clapped his friend on the shoulder sympathetically, but the tone in his voice remained serious. "For now we're safe. Zabella's got the game. If we just stick together and stay in crowded public places we'll be fine. Our first step should be to return to the practice so Zabella doesn't start thinking we're onto him. Then we'll go to the student union—you know, hide in plain sight—grab a bite to eat, and come back to the arena for the game."

Davis nodded at the Hardys. He pushed open the door leading into the arena and walked through. Frank and Joe followed. "It makes sense," Davis agreed. "But I don't think I can sit through a game knowing Zabella's going to come after us."

"But we've got to draw him out," Frank said. "We don't have any hard evidence. So whether we like it or not we're just going to have to wait for Zabella to make his move."

"So far, so good," Joe said to his brother and Davis. "With so many people on campus for the game, the student union was the perfect place to get lost in a crowd." The three guys were standing in front of the main entrance to the arena. They were waiting for the athletic director, Ray Crawford, because they were to be his guests at the game.

"Good to see you again," a man said as he approached. "Ray Crawford!" he announced, his hand extended. "It's nice to get a chance to sit down for a while with you," he said to Davis. "And you guys as well."

"Always a pleasure, sir," Davis answered, shaking the athletic director's hand. The Hardys nodded hellos.

"We'd better hurry," the athletic director continued. "I want you to join the team in the locker room. Follow me." The athletic director maneuvered through the crowd filing into the arena, then led Davis and the Hardys into the lobby and through a door marked Personnel Only.

"The locker rooms were built into the basement. With all the service rooms and the like, a person can get lost down here," Crawford explained as they descended a flight of stairs.

"And with the construction work going on to connect the arena with the sports complex additions, it's a real maze."

After a few twists and turns past roped-off corridors and dark tunnels, the group reached the Bayport locker room.

"Here we are," the athletic director announced, pushing open the door. Walking into the crowded locker room a step behind Frank and Davis, Joe noticed Zabella huddled with Turbo and another man in the coach's small office. They were talking in hushed tones.

As Frank and Davis moved off with the athletic director into another part of the locker area, Joe kept his eyes on the coach's office.

When the third man in the office turned and faced the locker room, a chill ran down his spine. It was one of the guys who had attacked Davis at the Pit! Keeping his eyes on the office, Joe moved over to Davis and Frank. They were standing at the far end of the locker room as the team gathered for the pregame pep talk.

Joe was about to mention the third man to Frank when the man quickly left the locker room and Zabella came out of his office to address the team.

"Okay, guys!" Zabella shouted. The players stared eagerly at their coach. "You know what this game means—the championship." Zabella clapped his hands and pointed at the door. "So go out on that court, play hard, and win!"

As the players started getting up from the benches and heading for the door, Frank glanced at the athletic director, who was frowning. Probably because Zabella hadn't even mentioned Coach Whiteside, Frank thought.

Just then another voice addressed the team. It was Brundige. "Fellas," he said, and the players turned toward him. "Wait a second. It's been a tough week for all of us." Brundige glanced in Coach Zabella's direction. "But let's not forget Coach Whiteside. Do your best for him! I know he'd appreciate it."

At this the players whooped loudly. "Yeah," one player yelled as the team ran out of the locker room. "Let's win the game for Stormin' Norman!"

Following behind with Ray Crawford, Frank saw the athletic director smile in Brundige's direction. "Now, that's the kind of loyalty I like," Crawford said quietly to himself.

"Excuse me for a minute, guys," Ray Crawford shouted over the din of the rocking arena. The athletic director stood up and smiled as he glanced around at the crowd. It was just minutes before tip-off. Crawford, Davis, and the Hardys were right beside the Bayport bench.

"I've got to talk to the announcer," Crawford

said. Frank followed the stockily built Crawford with his eyes as the man walked over to the game officials.

Glancing toward the court, Frank saw both teams running layup drills and stretching in preparation for the game. The capacity crowd was abuzz with anticipation. As the players ended their drills and headed back to their benches, the lights in the arena went off. One spotlight shone directly on center court. Then a young woman stepped into the circle of light, a microphone in her hand.

"Ladies and gentlemen," a voice boomed over the PA, "please rise for the national anthem." Frank and the rest of the crowd stood as the singer began. Cheers started building as she finished. Frank then saw the athletic director escort the singer off the floor. Taking the microphone from her, Crawford returned to the spotlight. A hush fell over the arena as Crawford addressed the crowd.

"Thank you for coming," Frank heard Crawford say. "I'll keep this brief since we all want to get on with this exciting contest. But first I'd like us all to take a moment to remember Coach Norman Whiteside."

Looking out at the fans, Frank saw most bow their heads. Crawford continued. "In the heat of battle, we all want to win. But let me just share with you the words of one of our assistant coaches, Stan Brundige, who told the team to play hard for Coach Whiteside. I applaud Mr. Brundige and call on all of you—players, coaches, and fans alike—to think of Coach Whiteside, who loved basketball more than anything. Thank you!"

To loud cheers, the athletic director walked toward his seat next to Davis as the lights came back on and the players took the court.

"The way Crawford spoke about the coach," Davis said, turning to Frank, "I sure hope we find out he wasn't really involved in anything illegal."

"I agree," Frank answered as the athletic director took his seat. "Nice speech, sir," Frank told him, smiling.

The athletic director nodded. "I meant every word. Even though Coach W could be difficult, he cared about the school and his players. I'm sorry," Crawford added, addressing Davis, "that you didn't get a chance to play for him. But I do hope you'll be coming to Bayport."

Frank saw his friend's eyes darken slightly. "I'm just not sure yet," Davis said. He turned away from the director, embarrassed.

"I know, son," Crawford answered sympathetically. "With Coach W's death and all, I can imagine your confusion." He patted Davis on the knee. "I know whatever decision you make will be the right one. What's best for you is all that should count."

Frank could see Davis's face brighten.

On the court, the game started. The first half was a seesaw affair with the teams exchanging leads. Toward the end of the half, Packard built a ten-point lead.

"They're just not executing very well," Davis commented as a Bayport player threw a pass out-of-bounds. "And look," he added, pointing at Coach Zabella. "The coach doesn't seem to be into it at all. He should be playing a man-to-man defense. Packard's just killing his zone. And all he does is stare up at the stands."

"I noticed that, too," Joe said so that only Frank and Davis could hear. "He's got other things on his mind."

"We'll keep close tabs on him after the game," Frank whispered. Just then the buzzer sounded ending the half.

"That was a pretty poor half, huh, fellas?" the AD said. "I don't know what's going on with the team. But I aim to find out." He rose from his seat and hurried toward the exit. "Why don't you join me back in the locker room."

After following him there, Frank witnessed a chaotic scene. The players were squabbling with one another while Brundige stood impatiently waiting for Zabella to address the team. As

Frank quickly saw, the head coach was not around.

Crawford, followed by Joe and Davis, walked over to Brundige. Poking his head back out the door, Frank was startled to see Zabella sneaking down a passageway that led away from the locker room. Checking to see that no one noticed him, Frank took off after the coach.

Frank pursued Zabella down a dark corridor, lodging himself in a doorway as Zabella stopped and spoke to two men who'd just appeared from a stairwell. The three talked in hushed tones, making it impossible for Frank to hear what they were saying. But he did see Zabella wave his arms wildly as he pushed the men back toward the stairs. "Just do it," Zabella half shouted impatiently. "But wait for my signal!" The two men nodded as Zabella sprinted back up the dark corridor.

Frank pressed himself into the shadows, waiting breathlessly for the coach to pass and enter the locker room. As the echo of his footsteps grew fainter, Frank peered out cautiously. With Zabella in the locker room, Frank slipped in after him. Quietly he positioned himself next to Joe and Davis.

Zabella had started giving a rambling, incoherent pep talk. Glancing around the room, Frank saw everyone stare in surprise at the head coach. Suddenly Brundige stepped forward and addressed the Bayport squad.

"What Coach Zabella is trying to say," Brundige began in an upbeat tone of voice, "is that we can beat Packard. Execute the offense and play in-your-face defense, and the league championship will be ours. Now get out there!"

As the players filed out of the locker room with Zabella and Brundige behind them, Frank saw the athletic director smile at Brundige. Maybe he's reconsidering his decision about who should be head coach, Frank thought.

"You want a dog or some fries, Frank?" Davis asked as he and Joe headed out the door.

"You go on ahead. We'll get you something," Joe told Frank.

"Listen," Frank answered. He kept them a few paces behind Crawford and the team as they walked up a tight stairway toward the arena. "Zabella's planning something. He was late getting back to the locker room because he was talking with two guys."

Davis and the Hardys were almost at the top of steps. The players had already passed through the door and were in the tunnel leading onto the arena floor.

"What can Zabella do now?" Joe asked. "He's got a game to coach. Besides, a crowded arena isn't the most likely place to attack someone." Joe smiled at his brother. "Davis and I will be fine. You go and sit with Crawford. We'll hit the concession stand and be right back."

"Okay, fellas," Frank said after a few seconds, agreeing with his brother's reasoning. "I'll take a hot dog and a soda," he called over his shoulder as he jogged down the tunnel to catch up with the athletic director.

"Sure thing," Joe answered. He turned toward Davis. "If we go this way," he said, pointing down an adjacent corridor, "I think we'll come out by the concessions." The two had walked a few steps down the tunnel when they heard footsteps behind them.

"Don't move," Joe heard someone say. He whirled around and tensed at the sight of two masked men. "You're coming with us!"

"Who says?" Joe answered belligerently.

"This does!" one of the men responded. Joe and Davis's eyes widened in fear. The man was pointing an automatic pistol at their heads!

Chapter

15

"KEEP YOUR HANDS where I can see them," the gunman said menacingly. "Now, let's move it!" He pointed down the long tunnel he and his partner must have just come up. "This way." The second man stepped behind Joe and Davis and pushed them forward. Davis whirled around, an angry scowl on his face. "Hey—"

"All right! All right!" Joe said. Knowing that now wasn't the time to try anything rash, he held Davis back. "We'll come with you. Just don't get trigger-happy."

The two men forced them down one dark corridor after another. Joe tried to keep track of where they were but soon grew confused. Rounding a corner, they came to a passageway that had been roped off and marked Danger—Construction. It ended at a small tunnel with a ladder leading down into a subbasement.

"Stop here!" one gunman said. He motioned at his partner. "Go down first," he added, pointing at the ladder. "And if they try anything stupid when they come down, shoot 'em!"

The second man quickly descended the ladder. "Okay, now you!" the one in charge said, waving his pistol at Davis. As Davis started down the ladder, Joe slipped his right hand into the breast pocket of his shirt. With the gunman's attention focused on Davis, Joe dropped his temporary Bayport ID on the floor near the tunnel entrance as a marker in case Frank came to look for them.

"Now you!" the gunman barked, turning to Joe.

"No problem," Joe said. "We won't give you any trouble." Joe had been trying to place the gunman's voice, and then it hit him all at once. He was one of the basketball players from the Pit, Turbo's friend.

Stepping off the ladder, Joe found himself in a subbasement construction site, a dark, cramped series of corridors with pipes and electrical wiring crisscrossing the low ceiling. Davis, Joe noticed, had to hunch to remain standing.

As the gunman came down the steps, he motioned Joe and Davis down one of the corridors.

The two men then pushed Joe and Davis into a room off the corridor. Stepping in behind them, the first man motioned to his partner.

"Tie them up," he said, throwing his buddy a length of rope he'd taken off his belt. "Put out your hands," he told Joe and Davis.

The second man bound their hands and pushed them to the floor. "There," he said as he finished binding Joe's feet.

With their hands and feet tied, Joe and Davis sat propped up against a wall.

"That'll do," the first gunman said. "Now for the explosives."

"Explosives?" Joe gasped.

"Yeah," the gunman said. He had bent over and was placing a small device in a crack at the base of the wall. "You saw who killed the old coach, now you've got to die, too."

"But I didn't see—" Davis exclaimed.

"Talk all you want," the gunman interrupted. "No one will hear you down here." The two masked men shared an evil laugh.

"Tell me one thing," Joe asked. "You're Turbo's buddies, aren't you?"

"Yeah, we are," the gunman answered. "Turbo won't have to worry about you," he said to Davis, "taking his spot on the team now, will he?"

Davis narrowed his eyes, seething with anger.

"Try not to sweat it, fellas," the gunman said

mockingly. "It'll be over quick." As his partner climbed back up the ladder, the first gunman went on. "In a few minutes you'll be dead. We're going to detonate the bomb by remote control when the cheering is at its loudest. You'll be dead and buried and no one will know."

Joe and Davis could only stare at the gunman.

"Listen carefully to the game, boys," he said, scrambling up the ladder. "The next cheer you hear will probably be your last."

"I sure hope Bayport can cut into this lead," Frank said to Ray Crawford. He and the athletic director had settled back in their seats just as the second half got under way.

"Me, too, son," Crawford answered, intently watching the action on the court. "All right!" Crawford yelled with all the other Lancer fans as a Bayport shot flew through the hoop.

After a few minutes into the third quarter, Bayport had cut the Packard lead to six. Frank was growing more and more uneasy—Joe and Davis had been gone too long. Noticing Frank straining to look up the aisle, Crawford laughed. "It could take your friends a while," he said. "The lines get long. Just enjoy the game."

"Okay, sir," Frank agreed, taking a last glance toward the exit before turning his attention back to the court. Just then Frank noticed two men sit down to the right of the Bayport bench, very close to Coach Zabella. Frank saw one of them nod and give the coach a thumbs-up sign.

Frank rose from his seat: "I'm going to look for Joe and Davis," he told the athletic director calmly. Despite his outward cool, Frank's mind was racing as he bounded up the aisle.

A quick glance at the concession stand confirmed his suspicions. No Joe or Davis. Breaking into a nervous sweat, he sprinted down a corridor leading to the locker area. Still no sign of either his brother or Davis.

Frank peered down one of the dark passageways that led off the main corridor, then cautiously entered it. It ran past a construction tunnel that had been roped off. Reaching the tunnel entrance, Frank saw a small white object on the floor.

"What's this?" he said to himself, bending to pick it up. His eyes opened wide. It was Joe's ID card. Frank knew then that Joe and Davis must be in trouble.

Frank scanned the area, his heart pumping wildly, then began to climb down the ladder.

By the last rung, Frank's eyes had adjusted to the dark, and he peered cautiously down each of the subbasement tunnels leading off into the gloom. "It's like a maze," he muttered. Frank felt the whole subbasement vibrate with each loud cheer from the arena above. He finally chose one of the tunnels and began to walk down it, his footsteps echoing.

"Is someone down here?" Frank heard a faint voice shout.

"Joe? Is that you?"

"Yeah, Frank!" Joe said frantically. "You've got to get to us quick. Follow my voice!" Joe kept talking, and Frank was able to identify the room the two were in.

Stepping over the debris blocking the opening to the room, Frank rushed over to Joe and Davis and bent to untie them.

"Forget about the ropes," Joe said, his face shiny with sweat. "There's a bomb in here!"

Joe motioned with his head at the crack in the wall. "And it could go off at the next loud cheer!"

As Frank followed Joe's eyes to the small electrical device in the wall, the subbasement room suddenly shook violently. Davis sucked in a breath. The roar coming from the arena above was building to a crescendo.

His eyes locked on the bomb, Frank froze, waiting to see if it would explode!

Chapter

16

As THE ROAR SUBSIDED the guys let out a collective sigh of relief.

"I thought for sure that was it," Davis said quietly. "But now—"

"I've got to defuse this bomb," Frank said, interrupting his friend. He knelt in front of the explosive device. "We're not out of the woods yet."

Joe and Davis were tense as Frank gave the device a quick once-over. "Simple enough," he said after a minute. "There's no booby trap. I'll just remove the remote connection wire—like this." He pulled a wire from the plastic explosive and showed it to Joe and Davis. "Voilà, no bomb."

138

"Great job!" Joe exclaimed. "Now, how about a hand with these ropes."

"Sure thing." Frank bent over and untied the two. Joe and Davis got up, rubbing their wrists where the ropes had cut into their skin.

The Hardys and Davis made their way through the debris in the tunnel and scrambled up the ladder. After stepping into the corridor above the subbasement, Frank leaned down into the opening to give Joe and Davis a hand.

"We'd better pull the plug on these guys now," Frank said once the other two were up. "Let's find them."

"I don't think that'll be a problem, Frank," Joe said in a low, serious tone. "They've found us. Look." Joe pointed down the corridor.

Frank whirled around. Blocking the exit were the gunmen who'd abducted Joe and Davis accompanied by a third man. They were striding menacingly toward the guys.

"You've got more lives than a cat," the lead man said. "But now we're going to finish you for good." They leaped toward Davis and the Hardys. Running past his brother, Joe rushed the head attacker. While they grappled in the middle of the corridor, Frank and Davis met the other two with body blows and karate kicks.

The battle slowly turned in the Hardys' favor. Davis's pistonlike punches had his assailant cowering. With slashing kicks and fierce punches,

Frank and Joe backed their opponents toward the entrance where they'd just come in.

"Don't mess with us anymore," Davis yelled. Just then a half-dozen security guards burst through the doorway.

"All right, break it up!" one guard said. He brandished a nightstick while the others surrounded the group.

"These guys jumped us," the guy Frank had overpowered claimed. "They're Packard fans."

"That's garbage," Joe yelled, trying to pull away from the guard who'd taken his arm.

Frank sucked in a deep breath, then started to explain everything as calmly as he could. He could tell the guard thought his story was made up.

The head security man scratched his head. "I guess we'd better take in the whole lot of them." He gestured to his men. "Come on."

Joe rolled his eyes but followed silently as the guards escorted them to the passageway leading toward the arena. They stopped at the threshold, where they could see part of the court. They arrived just as the Bayport team won the game and the crowd erupted in jubilant cheers.

Suddenly Joe got a bright idea. He yelled out, "Hey, Zabella!"

Despite the noise of the crowd, Zabella heard his name being called. He turned in their direction. When he saw the Hardys and Davis alive and well, his jaw dropped.

Joe didn't wait a second longer. He broke away from the security men and pushed his way through the crowd, reaching Zabella before the guards could stop him.

"There's nowhere to run, Coach," Joe said sternly. "Your buddies are in custody. And now it's your turn."

Zabella grew pale as he glanced up the aisle and saw his henchmen with security. By now Turbo had come to his side.

"What's going on?" Joe heard Ray Crawford shout. Crawford and Stan Brundige started moving through the crowd. Just then the head security man arrived, too, with Frank and Davis in tow.

"Sir," Joe said to the athletic director, "I'll explain everything later, but Zabella murdered Coach Whiteside—and tried to kill Davis and me, too."

"What do you mean?" Crawford asked, aghast.

"He's telling the truth," Frank yelled, pushing forward. "And we can prove it."

Zabella shot Frank a furious glance. His eyes were bulging, and the veins in his head looked ready to explode. The security man had to hold him back to keep him from charging Frank.

"*You* cost me my dream," he snapped.

"What do you mean?" Ray Crawford said sternly. He stepped in between Zabella and Frank. Frank could see that the athletic director was still stunned by the events.

"I'm not saying another word until I speak to my attorney," Zabella said defiantly. "You haven't got a thing on me."

Just then Joe walked up to Turbo, who was standing behind Zabella. "We can ID your car as the one that tried to run us off the road," he whispered into Turbo's ear. "You might want to cooperate." Hearing that, the player shook violently.

"He did it, Mr. Crawford," Turbo blurted out. "He killed Coach Whiteside." At this Zabella lunged for Turbo. While the head security guard subdued Zabella, Turbo kept talking. "He gave the coach the fake pills and then tried to set up Coach Brundige by planting them in his office. I had nothing to do with it, sir. You've got to believe me."

"Nothing to do with it." Zabella smiled meanly. "You and your buddies only tried to run these kids off the road." Zabella nodded toward Frank, Joe, and Davis. "*Your* buddies threatened them and set the fire in the dorm. And *you* tried to lure them onto a demolition site. Yeah. You're real innocent all right."

"Mr. Crawford! What's going on?" someone shouted from the growing crowd surrounding

142

them. The whole group turned. A throng of reporters were fighting their way toward them.

"Get these two out of here," the athletic director said to the guard, gesturing toward Zabella and Turbo. He positioned himself in front of the oncoming reporters as the security man led the coach and Turbo off the court.

"No problem here, folks," Crawford said in a loud voice. "We'll have a press conference in a few minutes. But for now, clear out." Saying this, Crawford herded Frank, Joe, Davis, and Brundige to Zabella's small office in the Bayport locker room and shut the door behind them.

"Now, you guys better fill me in on what's happened," Crawford demanded. "Those vultures are going to want a story."

"Okay now, fellas, settle down," Ray Crawford addressed the raucous crowd of reporters gathered in front of him. "Here's what we know at this time. Coach Zabella and one of our players, Turbo Thomson, have been arrested."

"For what?" a reporter yelled from the back of the press room.

"The murder of Coach Whiteside," the athletic director answered calmly. A buzz of excitement surged through the room. "Not to mention the attempted murder of a recruit, Davis Johns, and his friends Frank and Joe Hardy."

THE HARDY BOYS CASEFILES

Reporters fired questions at the athletic director. "Quiet down!" he shouted. "Let me introduce Frank and Joe Hardy. They were instrumental in solving the case and apprehending Zabella and Turbo." Motioning to Frank, Crawford stepped back and pointed at the cluster of microphones mounted on the podium. Frank walked forward.

"It happened this way," he began, squinting into the bright lights of the TV cameras. "Eddie Zabella murdered Coach Whiteside."

"Murdered him?" one repeated in disbelief.

"Yes," Frank answered.

Ray Crawford nodded at Frank. "Go ahead, son. Tell them the whole story."

Frank returned the nod and continued. "Zabella had wanted Whiteside's job for years, but he knew Coach Brundige had seniority," Frank said, glancing over at the assistant coach standing on his left with Davis, "Zabella worried that Whiteside was grooming Brundige to take over. He knew the coach was getting sicker and sicker, so he planted fake pills to make sure Whiteside wouldn't recover from his next heart attack."

"This is unbelievable," one reporter exclaimed.

"But true," Frank responded. "Zabella also planted fake pills in Brundige's office in order to divert suspicion and incriminate Brundige."

"How did you guys get involved," the reporter asked.

"We were visiting the campus with Davis," Frank said, motioning toward his friend. "We happened to be looking for Whiteside just after his fatal attack. Zabella thought we saw him, so he came after us." Frank looked at Joe. "My brother will fill you in on those details."

Frank took a step back from the podium and pushed his brother toward it. Joe bent toward the microphones.

"Zabella hired some of Turbo Thomson's buddies to frighten us off," Joe began. "When we weren't so easily scared, they tried to kill us."

The reporters began shouting questions all at once.

"But there's more," Joe added, raising his voice a notch to get everyone's attention. "There was another person involved." The room was silent. Even Brundige and the athletic director appeared shocked. Joe leaned forward and peered into the camera lights. "Coach Trevanian," he said. Trevanian had been standing in the back of the room, leaning against a wall. "Would you care to explain about the ten thousand dollars you sent Davis?"

All eyes turned to the back of the room. The blood left the Packard coach's face. "I—I—" he stammered. "All right. I sent the money, trying to make Davis think Bayport and Whiteside were corrupt."

"What about those allegations you made against Coach Whiteside?" a reporter called out. "Were they true?"

"Let me say now that Coach Whiteside was always aboveboard," Trevanian answered quickly. "He was involved in no illegal activities that I know of. You've got to understand," he continued, wringing his hands as he spoke, "I was under a lot pressure to win. And I certainly didn't want Bayport to get another top recruit. I know I was wrong. In fact, I've already contacted the CBA and confessed the whole thing."

"Coach T, Coach T—" the reporters shouted in unison. "Will you answer some questions?"

"I will issue a statement through my attorney," Trevanian said. "Now I think . . ."

As Trevanian was about to continue, Ray Crawford stepped past Frank and Joe to the podium and addressed the room. "Please give Coach Trevanian some courtesy, fellas. He'll answer questions when he's ready." Trevanian shot a thankful glance at the Bayport athletic director and quickly hurried out of the room.

Everyone turned back to Crawford.

"We have another announcement to make," the athletic director went on. "And this one is a plus for the Bayport program." Crawford turned to Assistant Coach Brundige. "Stan, will you come up here?"

Frank, Joe, and Davis took a step back so Brundige could stand next to the athletic director.

"Stan Brundige will be the next head coach of the Bayport Lancers." Frank saw almost everyone in the room nod his head in approval. "I've watched Stan handle himself with dignity during these past few tumultuous days. He's deeply committed to the program and most importantly to the kids." Crawford clapped Brundige on the shoulder with his left hand. "Now. I'll let *Head* Coach Brundige say a few words."

Brundige stepped in front of the microphones. "Thank you, Ray," Brundige began, a wide smile on his face. "I just want to make one announcement. The team's been through some tough times, but I know we've got the character to put them behind us. And to start what I hope will be a long tenure here, I'm announcing that Davis Johns—a local product, as you know—has agreed to attend Bayport in the fall."

As the reporters clapped, Frank looked at his friend. Davis, too, was beaming. He leaned over and whispered in Frank's ear. "Brundige is a good man and a good coach. I think I'm going to like it here." He draped his arms on the shoulders of Frank and Joe. "And I owe it all to you guys. Thanks."

"No sweat," Frank said, beaming.

"One last thing," Coach Brundige said. He turned to Frank and Joe and then addressed the reporters with a laugh. "These two detectives are pretty fair players themselves, I understand," he said, pointing at the Hardys. "When they're ready for college, tryouts await."

Frank and Joe both laughed. Then Frank pushed Davis up to the podium. "We'll leave the hoop heroics to Davis," he said.

Frank and Joe smiled as their friend and Brundige stepped into the bright lights of big-time college hoops.

"College ball, huh?" Joe whispered to his brother. "Sounds appealing."

Frank just kept laughing. "We'd best stick to what we know. As basketball players, we make great detectives!"

Frank and Joe's next case:

Frank and Joe's friend Phil Cohen, Bayport High's resident electronics whiz, has landed a job at Futron, a manufacturer of highly classified, high-tech military equipment. But the work is loaded with occupational hazards. The Hardys learn just how hazardous when both Phil and his boss disappear . . . leaving only a trail of blood behind. The enormous significance of the case becomes clear when the boys come face-to-face with the Gray Man, a top operative for the ultrasecret Network. The investigation leads Frank and Joe from kidnapping to murder . . . and ultimately to distant, dangerous shores, where a massive threat to global security is waiting to explode . . . in *Blown Away,* Case #108 in The Hardy Boys Case-files™.

THE HARDY BOYS CASEFILES

☐ #1: DEAD ON TARGET	73992-1/$3.99		☐ #73: BAD RAP	73109-2/$3.99
☐ #2: EVIL, INC.	73668-X/$3.75		☐ #74: ROAD PIRATES	73110-6/$3.99
☐ #3: CULT OF CRIME	68726-3/$3.99		☐ #75: NO WAY OUT	73111-4/$3.99
☐ #4: THE LAZARUS PLOT	73995-6/$3.75		☐ #76: TAGGED FOR TERROR	73112-2/$3.99
☐ #5: EDGE OF DESTRUCTION	73669-8/$3.99		☐ #77: SURVIVAL RUN	79461-2/$3.99
☐ #6: THE CROWNING OF TERROR	73670-1/$3.50		☐ #78: THE PACIFIC CONSPIRACY	79462-0/$3.99
☐ #7: DEATHGAME	73672-8/$3.99		☐ #79: DANGER UNLIMITED	79463-9/$3.99
☐ #8: SEE NO EVIL	73673-6/$3.50		☐ #80: DEAD OF NIGHT	79464-7/$3.99
☐ #9: THE GENIUS THIEVES	73674-4/$3.50		☐ #81: SHEER TERROR	79465-5/$3.99
☐ #12: PERFECT GETAWAY	73675-2/$3.50		☐ #82: POISONED PARADISE	79466-3/$3.99
☐ #14: TOO MANY TRAITORS	73677-9/$3.50		☐ #83: TOXIC REVENGE	79467-1/$3.99
☐ #32: BLOOD MONEY	74665-0/$3.50		☐ #84: FALSE ALARM	79468-X/$3.99
☐ #35: THE DEAD SEASON	74105-5/$3.50		☐ #85: WINNER TAKE ALL	79469-8/$3.99
☐ #41: HIGHWAY ROBBERY	70038-3/$3.75		☐ #86: VIRTUAL VILLAINY	79470-1/$3.99
☐ #44: CASTLE FEAR	74615-4/$3.75		☐ #87: DEAD MAN IN DEADWOOD	79471-X/$3.99
☐ #45: IN SELF-DEFENSE	70042-1/$3.75		☐ #88: INFERNO OF FEAR	79472-8/$3.99
☐ #47: FLIGHT INTO DANGER	70044-8/$3.99		☐ #89: DARKNESS FALLS	79473-6/$3.99
☐ #49: DIRTY DEEDS	70046-4/$3.99		☐ #90: DEADLY ENGAGEMENT	79474-4/$3.99
☐ #50: POWER PLAY	70047-2/$3.99		☐ #91: HOT WHEELS	79475-2/$3.99
☐ #53: WEB OF HORROR	73089-4/$3.99		☐ #92: SABOTAGE AT SEA	79476-0/$3.99
☐ #54: DEEP TROUBLE	73090-8/$3.99		☐ #93: MISSION: MAYHEM	88204-X/$3.99
☐ #55: BEYOND THE LAW	73091-6/$3.50		☐ #94: A TASTE FOR TERROR	88205-8/$3.99
☐ #56: HEIGHT OF DANGER	73092-4/$3.99		☐ #95: ILLEGAL PROCEDURE	88206-6/$3.99
☐ #57: TERROR ON TRACK	73093-2/$3.99		☐ #96: AGAINST ALL ODDS	88207-4/$3.99
☐ #60: DEADFALL	73096-7/$3.75		☐ #97: PURE EVIL	88208-2/$3.99
☐ #61: GRAVE DANGER	73097-5/$3.99		☐ #98: MURDER BY MAGIC	88209-0/$3.99
☐ #62: FINAL GAMBIT	73098-3/$3.75		☐ #99: FRAME-UP	88210-4/$3.99
☐ #63: COLD SWEAT	73099-1/$3.75		☐ #100: TRUE THRILLER	88211-2/$3.99
☐ #64: ENDANGERED SPECIES	73100-9/$3.99		☐ #101: PEAK OF DANGER	88212-0/$3.99
☐ #65: NO MERCY	73101-7/$3.99		☐ #102: WRONG SIDE OF THE LAW	88213-9/$3.99
☐ #66: THE PHOENIX EQUATION	73102-5/$3.99		☐ #103: CAMPAIGN OF CRIME	88214-7/$3.99
☐ #68: ROUGH RIDING	73104-1/$3.75		☐ #104: WILD WHEELS	88215-5/$3.99
☐ #69: MAYHEM IN MOTION	73105-X/$3.75		☐ #105: LAW OF THE JUNGLE	50428-2/$3.99
☐ #71: REAL HORROR	73107-6/$3.99		☐ #106: SHOCK JOCK	50429-0/$3.99
☐ #72: SCREAMERS	73108-4/$3.75		☐ #107: FAST BREAK	50430-4/$3.99

Simon & Schuster Mail Order
200 Old Tappan Rd., Old Tappan, N.J. 07675

Please send me the books I have checked above. I am enclosing $_____ (please add $0.75 to cover the postage and handling for each order. Please add appropriate sales tax). Send check or money order--no cash or C.O.D.'s please. Allow up to six weeks for delivery. For purchase over $10.00 you may use VISA: card number, expiration date and customer signature must be included.

Name _____

Address _____

City _____ State/Zip _____

VISA Card # _____ Exp.Date _____

Signature _____ 762-30